In the Heat of the Night

SUSANNE BELLAMY

ISBN:
978-0-6485275-1-0:

DEDICATION

For Gillian, best of big sisters. Love you, sis

In the Heat of the Night is part of a group writing venture, 'Bindarra Creek A Town Reborn'. For details on the other books in this series, please visit our website: https://bindarracreekromance.com

..

Chapter 1

Kel Jones parked his car in front of the antiques shop, catching a glimpse through the window of his deputy fire captain, Dodge Myers, serving a customer.

After the awful weather and flooding last month, the mild start to August was a blessing.

Kel tipped his face towards the sun, enjoying the warmth of a cloudless winter day. He added the pleasant weather to the fact Wednesdays in Bindarra Creek meant a lunch of Thea Levonis' wonderful cooking.

And bantering with Thalia at the register.

Not that Kel was interested in *that* way in the good Greek daughter of Thea and Stavros. But stirring Thalia to lose her cool was fun, and helped him to forget for a short time that August held an anniversary he hated.

He lengthened his stride, but in four years, he hadn't succeeded in outrunning his memory.

He turned in at the open door of the Cyprus Café and sniffed the air.

Moussaka, I'll bet my bottom dollar.

He stopped in front of the register and waited for his turn. Bunting of Greek and Australian flags hung along freshly-painted blue and white walls, making the red seats in the booths along the far wall stand out.

Behind the counter, Thalia Levonis took a tray of baklava from the display cabinet and picked up a pair of tongs. She called "Goodbye, see you next week" to the Wednesday lunch club ladies and smiled at her next customer. "How many pieces would you like, Esther—sorry, Mrs Ainslie?"

Esther took a lavender-coloured notebook from her handbag and consulted it. "Seven—no, better make it eight please. Ty Devereaux is joining us tonight."

"Annie's fiancé? Wow, does your son-in-law-to-be know he's coming into a book club with all women?"

Kel's ears pricked at mention of the newest addition to Bindarra's legal community. With Ty making the permanent move to town, Kel intended to approach him to join the Fire and Rescue service. Kel's stomach rumbled.

After lunch.

He took out his phone and added a reminder to call Ty while Thalia served Esther.

"He knows and is looking forward to lively discussion. Maybe we'll be able to encourage a few more men to join once he's braved the first meeting." She closed her notebook and slipped it back into her handbag. "I wonder if I should get something else for nibbles?"

"Men usually like to eat more than women."

Esther tapped a finger over her lips, staring at the displays. She caught Kel's eye and smiled. "Go ahead and serve the next customer while I have another think, dear."

"No problem, Mrs Ainslie." Thalia closed the cabinet door and turned to Kel.

"What can I do for you?"

***

The dark blue eyes of Bindarra Creek's fire brigade captain sent tremors fluttering in her stomach. Then reality crashed around her. Once upon a time—*about ten women ago*—she had thought she could be the woman who won his sole attention.

"Ah, Thali, that's a loaded question for a beautiful woman to ask a man." He smiled, the same smile he offered every female in Bindarra Creek, whether they were eight or eighty. The smile that said he appreciated every one of them. The smile that said they were beautiful . . . *but not for him, not in the long-term.*

Three dates is long-term for Kel Jones.

Thalia had never had even one date with him, and yet she probably reacted the same way other women did, felt the same stirring in the belly, like the heartburn of indigestion only not so easy to get over. It didn't help that she secretly liked the way he shortened her name; it rolled off his tongue like an endearment.

And that's absolutely not okay.

She wasn't even certain she liked him anymore.

Good luck to any woman who thought she could catch and keep Bindarra Creek's most eligible bachelor. Thalia no longer counted herself in their ranks.

"My name is Tha-li-a; three syllables with an a on the end." Her tone was snappy and she cut off a less than polite name for arrogant men, and Kel in particular.

This was Mama and Papa's café. Telling a customer he was an arrogant *vlaka* wouldn't be good for business. And Kel was a regular. Every Wednesday without fail. "Let me rephrase that. What would you like—from the cabinet or the menu?"

"Spoilsport." He turned his gaze to the blackboard above her head. "Something hot, with a touch of spicy heat." His gaze flicked back to her.

If he thinks he can charm me with that old cliché, he's got another think coming.

No, she didn't like him, or the way her body angled towards him, responding of its own accord. Thalia leaned on the counter beside the *bain-marie* and pressed her hands down hard. She refused to give him the satisfaction of showing the slightest interest.

Interest, awareness . . . desire.

Ten years of frustrated desire. Ten years of watching Kel date other women. Ten years of fantasising about him desiring her above all others.

Damn and blast the man, she wasn't going to waste another moment on him. "Let me know when you've decided what you want."

Thalia hoped Esther took as much time to select her cakes as she had taken to select books for the town library. Maybe Mama would return from the kitchen and deal with Captain *I'm-so-wonderful* Jones before Thalia had to talk to him again.

She checked to see if Esther had reached a decision and found her friend watching her, a curious expression in her gaze. She nodded once, as though filing something in her memory.

Shoot, had she been so preoccupied thinking about Kel, she missed hearing Esther's order?

"So, Mrs Ainslie, what looks good to you?"

"I'll take some of those *spanakopites* too. Seeing we now have a man attending our book club."

Kel turned to Esther. "Mrs Ainslie, never tell me you've opened up the ladies book club of Bindarra Creek to we poor intellectually starved men?"

"Wouldn't hurt you to come along, Kel. We discuss great books and stories to touch your heart."

"Fifty Shades, no thanks. I'm not into that stuff." A flicker of distaste crossed his face.

Thalia set the box of *spanakopites* on top of the glass cabinet.

So the fire captain would break hearts, but not rules.

She moved to the register and added the *spanakopites* to Esther's bill, all too aware of Kel's presence. He dominated the space, and her thoughts. "How do you know what *stuff* is in those books if you've never read them?"

Kel's mouth opened and closed. He looked like the fish her brother Nico had caught—

Thalia struggled not to laugh. That fish was family legend. When Nico was ten-years-old, he'd come close to catching the huge cod, the one every local fisherman had tried to catch. The one he'd lifted out of the river, dangling from his rod. The one that fell off the hook before he landed it and, with an indignant flick of its tail, disappeared in the swift-flowing waters of the Akuna River.

Kel, the cod. And no woman could land him. She pressed her lips together.

"Got me there, Thali—sorry, Tha-li-a. It's just what I've heard from some of BC's ladies."

Some of—

Other women. Of course. What did I ever see in this arrogant man?

Damn the man. With one comment, in the

space of a breath, he could turn her from laughter to wanting to flatten him.

Thalia folded her arms and pinned him with a Medusa-glare. "In *our* book club, we read good books in all sorts of genres. There are eight women, and Ty, Annie's fiancé, is joining us tonight for the first time. Everyone takes a turn to choose a book and each month we meet in the home of one of our members to discuss their choice. Tonight is Mrs Ainslie's turn to host."

"Our— You're in this book club too, are you?"

"Of course. It's my turn to host next month." Thalia carefully packed Esther's purchases in her shopping bag.

He leaned on the glass cabinet and watched her with a grin hot enough to melt Esther's *baklava*. "And what book have you chosen, Thalia? A modern Greek tragedy?"

"I did consider *Fire on the Water*, but I've always wanted to see the Silk Road, so that's what mine is about. It's written from a travel writer's perspective."

Kel's focus zeroed in on her, like Zeus, her brother's German Shepherd when he heard the word, *walk*. She didn't want Kel's attention, making her think of fairy tale happy-ever-afters. She didn't want him. Period.

But the idea of stirring Kel?

Almost as tempting as the idea of kissing him had been—before she outgrew her teenage fantasy. "One day I'm going to travel along parts of that route."

"With a tourist group." Kel wasn't asking. It was a statement, an assumption backed by a belief that Thalia wasn't a real traveller.

Not like him.

"Not with a group. I want to walk it, by myself for preference."

"You want to walk the Silk Road, you need to get fit." He leaned closer until he was in her face and his warm breath skated past her cheek. "That place isn't for arm-chair travellers or— " he broke off and smiled.

"Or what?" she demanded. "Women? Because we're the weaker sex? Because only a six-foot-tall man should travel such roads? Why, if I had—"

A rush of heat raced up her cheeks. Most times she kept her passion and dreams of travel under wraps, but Kel Jones brought out her fire.

Kel raised a hand. "Thalia, I don't consider women weak. Far from it. We have lots of women in both the rural fire brigades and the Fire and Rescue teams, and they're wonderful at their jobs. But on the Silk Road—there are areas where a lone woman would be seen as . . ."

"You don't think I'm strong enough."

A muscle jumped in his cheek.

"Weakness has nothing to do with it, Thalia. But you *are* a woman." He leaned even closer. The counter shrank until it felt like no barrier at all.

He was in her face, suddenly more serious than she'd ever seen him.

"I've been there. I've seen the locals and how they treat women. No matter what books you read, they'll never prepare you for the reality of life in those places. Every man there regards women as being created solely for their pleasure. And they've never heard of, let alone understand the concept of 'No'."

Thalia stared at him. The cold, hard implacable statement coming from Kel scared her more than she wanted to admit.

"Travel along the Silk Road is not for the faint-hearted." His voice was rough and biting and could clearly be heard in the hush that had descended in the café. "No lone woman is safe there. Not in some of the places that road passes through.

"You'd be in danger of assault—rape or murder."

Rape—murder . . . The words chilled her.

"Promise you won't do it, not alone—it would be a really bad decision. But Thali . . ."

Thalia struggled for breath against the dark images in her mind. Kel was right, dammit, but she wouldn't give him the satisfaction of saying so.

"I don't doubt you could walk the length of the Silk Road if you decided to."

Esther lifted her shopping bag onto the counter. "If you've finished sweet-talking Thalia, Kel, I'd like to finish my order."

"Sorry, Mrs Ainslie." Kel's standard one-size-fits-all smile slid into place.

With an effort, Thalia retreated to her customer-friendly face. "Was there anything else, Mrs Ainslie?"

Esther turned to Kel with a guileless smile that didn't fool Thalia. Esther's mild manner hid a backbone of steel. Whatever she'd decided was going to happen, would.

"Kel, why don't you join us this evening? You and Ty can band together and give us a male perspective on—"

Kel's voice and hands rose, rejecting Esther's invitation. "Whoa, Esther, much as I'd love to join you, I'm not—"

"Stop right there, Kel. I know you enjoy reading. When I went in to Penny Lane Bookshop to pick up the book for next month's meeting, Penny was opening her latest delivery for you. Adventure stories and biographies of famous explorers are top of your purchases."

Kel tutted and shook his head in mock dismay. "It's a sad day when a man can't trust his book shop owner to keep his secrets. I'll have a word to say next time I'm in Penny's shop."

Esther settled her handbag into the crook of her arm. "Ask her for a copy of that book about the Silk Road and join us next month. With your travels in Nepal I'm sure you could offer a unique perspective."

"I'm sure I could. Tell you what, Esther, the day Thalia joins the fire service is the day I'll come to your book club."

Thalia's BS radar pinged. She drew her five feet three inches onto tiptoes, rested both hands on the counter and leaned towards him. Her voice was steel covered in silk. "Is that so? Where do I sign up?"

Kel grinned, a pat-Thalia-on-the-head-like-a-good-little-girl grin that roused the ancient warrior in her blood.

The arrogant vlaka didn't believe she'd really join the Fire Service.

Fury beyond any Greek drama surged through Thalia. "You arrogant, egotistical, *think-you're-superior*—"

Customers at the nearest tables turned to see what had stirred the usually placid eldest daughter of Thea and Stavros Levonis. She was past caring.

Kel's pager went off.

Thalia snapped her mouth shut. Everyone knew what that meant—a fire or accident requiring his crew.

He looked at the screen. "Call-out—I've got to go. Come and see me at the station later today if you're serious about becoming a firefighter. If not—" The bantering tone vanished, replaced by his no-nonsense, professional, get-the-job-done voice. A voice that reassured, a voice that said 'Trust Me' in bold, confident capitals. A voice that sent tingles down her spine and reminded her why her teenage self had fallen in love with the fire captain.

He turned to Esther. "Enjoy your book discussion tonight." Kel strode through the doorway, out of sight before Thalia could think of a reply.

"He has no intention of coming to our book club, unless you were serious about signing onto his fire crew?" Esther paused, the fifty-dollar note halfway out of her purse, and settled a needle-sharp gaze on Thalia. "Were you?"

Thalia looked at the door Kel had exited through, as though he might be there listening for her answer, certain it had been nothing more than a throwaway line. "Maybe I will check it out, even if all I do is give Captain Jones a surprise. I like the idea of putting him off balance."

"Good for you, Thalia. And you can bring him along after you've signed up. No more of these all-male or all-female clubs. I'm all for inclusivity."

***

The alarm woop-wooped at Bindarra Creek Fire Station. Kel swallowed hard. The thought of Thalia alone on the Silk Road was enough to curdle the coffee in his gut.

He could see it far too clearly.

Her lush curves, her deep throated laughter, her fire and courage, at the mercy of some of the lecherous bastards he'd met in his travels. Shit, it didn't bear thinking of.

He had to do something to prevent her undertaking anything so damned foolhardy.

And why the hell this matters to me, I have no idea.

The scrape of heavy boots on concrete alerted him to the arrival of the first of his team. He read the print out and put personal thoughts out of his head until later. Connor Jacobs rocked in behind Lou Myers and Gabe, completing the crew needed to take the fire truck out.

Lou sat on a bench and pulled on her boots. "What have we got?"

Small bush fire." Kel took his jacket, helmet, and two-way radio from the locker and picked up the co-ordinates of the fire from the printer.

"I couldn't see any smoke on my way here." Connor picked up the keys and joined the rest of the crew beside the truck.

"The fire's not in town."

"Then why has it come to us instead of the rural guys?" Connor opened the door of the truck.

"They're already out on call."

Mandy Kaminsky raced into the station. Their newest member was breathing hard and pink-cheeked.

Kel stopped, door handle in his grip. "It's fine, Mandy. We've got a team, but you can look after communications at this end and start on the report."

She waved a hand and sucked in a deep breath. "Sorry, my car's in the garage and I ran all the way from the shop. I'm not as fit as I thought."

"Worth focusing on next training day." Kel slid into his seat on the passenger side and looked across at Connor. "Everybody right to go?"

A chorus of checks greeted him. "Good. Head east on Mt Ingalls Road." He entered the details on the touch screen.

Mandy stepped into the road, checked for traffic and then gave them the all-clear.

Kel switched on the siren and lights.

Connor exited the station and turned right along the main east-west street. He glanced at the screen. "Looks like the fire is near Angus McGregor's place." He eased back at the intersection with Main Street. Mid-morning traffic stopped for the fire engine to pass.

Kel read the sparse information on the print out again. "Yeah, the rural crew at Glenmeer are already attending a grass fire the other side of their area so we were asked to cover the call-out."

"Not what I expected at the end of winter." Connor passed the eighty-kilometre road sign and increased speed.

"For all that rain last month and the local flooding, there's still plenty of long dry grass." Kel's phone rang. He pulled it from his pocket, looked at the screen, and accepted the call. "Angus, we're on our way, about five minutes from you now. How's it looking out there?"

A plume of white smoke rose above the trees, angling towards the west. When the truck topped a rise in the road, Kel tried to estimate the size of the fire. *Not big yet.*

"Not so close that the house is in danger, but the wind has picked up. It's turning the fire towards us. I've alerted the house sitters at Cam's place. They're keeping an eye on the back paddock where our properties meet." Angus' voice was calm and steady. In the background, a woman's voice rose, her words indistinct, but her tone agitated. "Claire's getting fidgety. Do you think we should leave now?"

Kel checked the time. "We're four minutes from you according to the GPS. Is your exit in danger?"

"It's clear at the moment, but I've got Claire to pack a bag. Ollie's anxious since the library fire, but Meg is sleeping. Look, I'll meet you at the entrance and bring you in. It'll be quicker if I lead you down through the paddocks. The fire front is close to the western dam, if you want to pump from that."

"Tell Claire to stay put for now. See you in a couple of minutes." He turned to his crew. "We'll be drafting from one of Angus' dams so get the suction hose out."

Lou gave him a corny salute. "Sure thing, Captain."

Kel grinned. "Lou Myers, when did you start getting so formal?"

Connor turned the truck onto the driveway of *Craigellachie*. Angus McGregor got behind the wheel of his ute and led the way through open gates. Both vehicles pulled up beside the dam.

The fire lacked fuel on scorched ground, but flames licked the base of a tall ghost gum.

Lou and Gabe unrolled the suction hose, dropping one end into the dam. Kel indicated where he wanted them to start. "We need to stop the fire getting into the canopy. This wind could whip it out of control."

Flames crackled in dry wood, danced along branches, jumped between bushes. Smoke spiralled where the fire had just caught, blazed in fat flames where it had taken hold. Burning scrub smelt like a hundred campfires, drawing the oxygen from the air, singeing the hair on Kel's skin when a wayward ember landed on his hand.

He turned to Angus and clapped one hand on his shoulder. "Thanks, mate. We'll take it from here. You get back to Claire and the children."

"She's over dealing with fires." Angus got in his ute.

Kel bent to the open window. "Water your roof, fill all your buckets—you know the drill. I'll phone if the situation here changes."

"Thanks." Angus turned the ute in a wide half-circle around the fire truck and headed back through the gate. Back to his family and his home.

Kel joined his team, pumping dam water, pushing back the hissing flames.

A branch, heavy with foliage, crashed from the ghost gum, scattering sparks and setting light to a small tree.

Wind gusted.

Flames streamed towards a stand of young eucalyptus trees.

Heat prickled Kel's nape, sweat ran down his back. He ignored both and joined Connor as he connected a hose to the tank of the appliance. "Ready on number two."

Kel picked up the nozzle and dragged the hose into position. "Ready." He opened a stream of water onto the new fire, extinguishing sparks before they could take hold.

Fighting fires was hot, hard, and dangerous, but adding worry over a wife and children threatened by fire?

That would be hell.

Chapter 2

The fire truck reversed into the station, its high-pitched beeps sending a strident warning. Connor switched the engine off and the crew climbed out, stretched, and began the clean-up and restocking process.

Kel collected his clipboard and phone from the dash and ran a hand through his hair, grimacing at the super-coat of soot over his black-streaked hands. "Who wants pizza when we're done here?"

Connor struggled out of his jacket and shook it. Two circles around his eyes from his safety goggles gleamed white on his shiny, soot-stained skin. "Think I'll head straight home."

"Lou, Gabe, what about you? Food and a quiet beer?"

Gabe opened the compartment and lifted out the wet suction hose. Mud from Angus' dam coated the base and strands of green water plants dropped as he set the hose-reel upright on the floor and gave it a kick towards the rear doors. "Yeah, count me in."

Lou looked at her sports watch. "Warren's looking after the twins. I should get back. Check he isn't tearing his hair out."

Mandy appeared in the office doorway and handed the checklist to Kel. His thumb left a grimy print on the top page.

Mandy pointed at the mark. "Soot, sweat, and ash—I don't think it'll catch on as the newest trend in skincare. Kel, the RFB captain from Glenmeer asked if you could call him when you've finished here."

"Thanks, Mandy. I'll do it now." Kel peeled off his overalls, washed his hands, and rang the Glenmeer captain. "Bert, how'd you go with that blaze?"

Bert Lamarr, a seasoned volunteer and now captain of the Glenmeer station, coughed before he answered. The dry cough of a firefighter not long returned from a smoky call-out. "Not a big one. Likely some idiot threw out a cigarette butt. Thanks for picking up the fire at the McGregor property. Any problems?"

"Touch-and-go when the wind turned, but Angus keeps a close eye on fuel load and he'd put a decent fire break in place between the homestead and the creek."

"Sensible bloke. He's had his share of fires over the years. Look, I just wanted to thank you and your crew. After the storm we had last month, it's a bit of a shock to find ourselves battling grass fires so early. We've got odd patches of dry grass and areas that are greening up almost side by side. It's weird. Crazy unseasonal rain."

"No worries, Bert. Yeah, we might have to start controlled burns early and reduce the fuel load. I'll call you in a day or two about burning off." When Kel finished the call he tossed his phone down, rubbed his gritty eyes and pushed away from the desk. The chair legs scraped over faded linoleum flooring and caught in a small rip. The edge of the seat dug into the back of his legs, right on a bruise he couldn't remember getting.

Voices—both female—filtered through from the staff kitchen. The words were indistinct but . . . He raised his head, and his nose twitched at the aroma. That's what he needed. *Coffee—strong, black, and keep-it-coming. Bless Mandy for putting the pot on.* He shuffled the paperwork to one side and made for the kitchen.

Mandy glanced up. "Looks like you've got a new recruit, Kel."

"Excellent. Who is it?" Kel couldn't see beyond the door.

A brief pause, the hint of curly black hair and then Thalia stepped into the room. Her chin rose, imperious as a warrior queen.

"Like I said before, where do I sign up, Captain?"

Kel folded his arms across his chest, holding back laughter at the diminutive figure of Thalia

Levonis in his fire station. Not only in his station, but demanding to join his crew. Certain she was playing him, he decided to play along. "Great. So you're serious?"

"Of course I am."

"In that case, Mandy, can you give Ms Levonis the hotline number and explain about the info pack and all that? Although maybe, since we've just returned from a call-out, we should *show* her what we do, starting with helping the crew clean off the appliance, which is what we call our fire truck." He stripped off his sweaty T-shirt, balled it and tossed it through the doorway onto his desk before strolling to the door.

Thalia gasped and her gaze fixed on his bare chest.

Kel grinned. *Two can play that game, Thali.*

"Coming, Tha-li-a?" He stressed the third syllable of her name and stood in front of her, one hand on the door beside her head.

Pink raced up her cheeks and her eyes flickered up, down to his bare chest and back up so fast he couldn't be certain. But he was almost sure he saw a flash of fire, a flicker of sensual awareness, and the promise of retribution in her eyes. Any one of those interested him. All three together? *Intriguing.*

He pulled the door wide open and gestured for her to lead the way into the garage. "So, when we get back from a call-out we wash down the vehicle, set out the hoses to dry, and replace them with dry hoses. Before we go home, the truck should be ready to go at the next call-out. If you're going to be joining us, you might as well start now." Kel winked at Connor.

"Hey guys, Thalia is going to become a firefighter." Connor's grin morphed into a lip-twitching attempt at an *I-mean-business* face. "Let's show her what the job involves. Here, Thalia, take this hose and wash the soot off the on side."

Thalia took the hose Connor handed her and studied the truck. "Which is the on side?"

"Opposite the off side."

Kel's crew had to work as a team—a single, cohesive unit that anticipated each other's moves. They'd worked together long enough to have rubbed off sharp edges and worked through personality differences. How would Thali respond?

Not that she's serious about joining. But Kel was curious how little Thali would react to Connor.

Her eyes narrowed. "And if I ask which is the off side you will tell me it's opposite the on side. Very funny—ha ha."

Connor pressed his lips together and spread his arms in fake commiseration. "Every firefighter knows these things."

Kel patted her shoulder. "Just point the nozzle at the truck and hose it down. Connor forgets that once upon a time, he had to learn all this too. Ready, Lou."

From the back of the station, Lou called out, "Tap's on."

"What?" Thalia turned towards Lou. Water burst through the nozzle and hit Connor square in the chest.

He spluttered and yelped and turned his back.

"Oh, I'm so sorry." Thalia fought to control the bucking hose.

Kel burst out laughing and scrambled for his phone. It would great payback for Connor's video of him tumbling down a mud bank and climbing out like the monster from the Black Lagoon. "Thalia, watch where you point that thing."

Thalia turned. Water hit Kel, the one-inch hose delivering a solid punch of cold, as only water coming through outside pipes in winter can be. Cold that set him gasping and blindly groping for the hose. He yanked it from her hands and yelled for Lou to shut off the water. The flow died to a drizzle.

Dripping wet, the two men eyed each other and then Thalia. They moved at the same moment. Kel was closer and reached her first. Wrapping an arm around her waist, he lifted her out of Connor's path.

Thalia squealed and struggled to escape. She pushed down on his arm and wriggled, her feet kicking his shins. "Put me down, you *vlaka*. Put me down."

Connor took a couple of squelching steps towards her, but Kel held him at bay. "Not fair, Kel."

"And I have seniority so I get first dibs. What the captain says, goes. Isn't that right, Thali?"

She tossed her head and pushed against the arm holding her waist in a tight grip. "*Chazo!*"

Kel didn't want to let her go, not when she was soft and warm and the scent of cinnamon teased his nose. He didn't want to release her . . . until her heel connected hard with his shin. "Ouch. Hey, I'm saving you here." He set her on her feet but stood between her and Connor.

Thalia spun to face him, hands making fists, cheeks pink, attitude with a capital A. "*Vlaka, chazo*".

"Why, Thali, that didn't sound very nice, especially about your superior officer."

"Superior, my ar—"

He was certain she'd offered him insults in return for his gallant rescue, but he knew no Greek. Putting a finger against her mouth, he stopped her response in English. "Tut, tut, such nice manners Esther said you had and here you are spitting like a cat. You'll have to learn to do as you're told if you're going to join my team."

He'd called her a cat, but she looked more

like a kitten with her beautiful dark brown eyes fixed on him, and pink lips he'd discovered were soft and plump when his finger had stopped her finishing her insult.

When had Thalia grown up into such an appealing little spitfire, tempestuous and tempting in ways that would be too distracting if he accepted her onto his team? "I don't think you'll be a good fit for my team if you can't do as you're told."

Bravery she had in spades. Discretion . . .

I'm going to walk the Silk Road . . .

He wondered about her crazy idea—crazy and defiant and strangely romantic.

"I do as my parents tell me, not what some big, muscly and full of—" She bit off what was destined to be another insult. "What some *chazo* who manhandles me tells me to do." Thalia folded her arms and gave him that look she'd levelled on him in the Cyprus Café. The look that challenged his every word. Her *laser-look,* he called it. It was intense, but damn it all, he liked being the focus of Thalia's attention.

Since when? The snide little voice in his head thumbed its nose at him, snapping him back to reality.

"If you join the fire service, you'll have to take orders. From me, from Lou, heck, maybe even from Connor if he's in charge of a call-out."

"You mean he gets to be the captain

sometimes? That everyone does?" She darted a look at Connor and Lou. "So—I'll get to be captain sometimes too, after I've done my training. Ha, I like that idea."

"God forbid, what have I agreed to?" The question escaped before he could censor it. What was it about Thalia that kicked down Kel's filters?

"Ah, now I see you're afraid." The little spitfire was smirking.

"What?" Had he zoned out in his fantasy of being the centre of her attention? "Afraid of what?"

"Me. You said you'd turn up at our book club the day I joined the fire service. Well here I am, ready to join up and you're trying to back out of your promise. I think the idea of our book club scares you."

Connor whooped and slapped his thighs. "Kel's joining the Bindarra Ladies Book Club? This I've got to see."

Kel flicked a look Connor had better interpret as *stay out of this or else*. "I'm not backing out of anything, Thalia. You haven't joined yet."

"You're nit-picking."

"I don't see your signature on any paper."

"Because you haven't given it to me and now you're saying I won't be a good fit for your crew."

She slapped a hand over her heart and suddenly Kel was all too aware of the swell of her breast above her demure work shirt, and the curves of her lush body any man worth the name would want to explore. Thalia stood before him, beautiful and diminutive and angry as a Greek goddess.

And all woman.

Something his body was all too eager to let him know. The irony didn't escape him. The instant *he* recognised her desirability, *she* made it abundantly clear how much she disliked him.

Double whammy. When had he ever had to convince a Bindarra female to go on a date?

Thalia's reaction puzzled him. Challenged him. Excited him.

"Well?" The challenge in her tone demanded the truth.

Kel just stood there. He had no clear idea what *truth* meant, not in the context of getting to know Thalia.

Work, he could handle. Work wasn't full of messy emotion and challenging, exciting women. "When you join the brigade, I'll turn up to your book club." He gave her a steady look. "A promise is a promise."

"Hah, exactly. Here I am, as I promised. Are you going to keep your side of the bargain?" Her hands fisted on her hips, a challenge in a hip-hugging, midnight-blue skirt.

He hauled in a deep breath, struggling for patience. You have to apply first." He ticked off items on his fingers. "Then you do an interview and only after that do you get to do the training. There are medical checks, and police checks. If you pass all of those, the final assessment is a physical. It's fairly strict to become a firefighter."

She nodded, a single nod, decisive and strong. She wouldn't fail. "Fine. I'll download whatever forms I need tonight and send them in. And this time next month, *Captain* Jones, you're going to honour your promise."

"This time next month I'll honour my promise. But you have to apply first."

She headed around the front of the truck, but stopped and looked back at him. Mischief danced in her eyes. "I suggest you take yourself down to Penny Lane's book shop and get that book I chose, because next month, I'll be accepted. Just you see."

Kel was beginning to understand that Thalia Levonis was very focused. When she decided on something, she would keep at it.

She wouldn't complete her training in a month, but he wasn't about to tell her. Recruits weren't so thick on the ground that he'd refuse her. If she was prepared to join his fire crew to get him to her book club, he would go, and gladly.

Elemental personality and all. And if he didn't survive her fire and fury?

It would be a damned fine way to go.

Chapter 3

Thalia sat back in one of Esther's sleek armchairs and sipped her wine, well aware she wasn't contributing as much as usual to the discussion of the book Esther had chosen. It wasn't that she disliked the book. The setting of Sydney in the 1960s, and the problems that beset the building of the Opera House were fascinating. And she had plenty to say about the shell motif running through the story. *Or she had when she'd been reading it.*

But the image of Kel Jones minus his shirt— *and wet, Thalia, don't forget the slide of water over his chest*—consumed her. And the memory of being plastered against him. The heat of his body against her back, the ripple of arm muscle pinning her to him as he moved her away from Connor's revenge, the . . .

"What do you think, Thalia?"

Seven pairs of eyes turned towards her. Heat ran up her neck. "About—I'm sorry. What were we talking about?"

Esther and Caroline Joy shared a look with one another, one that seemed to know what she'd been daydreaming about. Esther smiled. "Never mind, dear. You've got a lot on your mind at the moment. Did you pick up the application form for the fire brigade?"

A chorus of voices rose, questions in tones of shock, dismay and intrigue, from, "You're joining the fire brigade?" to "Why?"

"Are you serious, Thalia?" Claire McGregor leaned forward, her fingernails digging into the padded arms of the chair. "Do you have *any* idea what it's like, facing a raging fire?"

Goose bumps crawled down Thalia's spine. If not for people like Kel risking their safety and their lives for others, Claire might not be sitting here today and Angus could have lost both his son and the woman he loved in the library fire a couple of years earlier.

Thalia held up both hands, and the comments died down. "I'm only just realising how much we depend on our fire services, and . . . I know this will seem sudden to you. It surprised me too." She rested both hands on her lap to hide their trembling.

The memory of flames and scorching heat pouring out of the library basement weren't easy to forget, even from across the road where she'd stood with her brother and watched in fear as Claire and Ollie were pulled out of that inferno.

"I went to the fire station and was told I had to apply online. I did that before I came here, and now I have to wait until they do background checks and . . . oh, lots of things. The main thing is I've started the process."

"So where is Kel Jones? He promised he'd come when you signed up."

A shrewd glint lit Esther's eyes. She was stirring the gossip pot and Thalia wondered why. Esther was usually so gossip-averse, but she'd chosen to target Kel tonight.

And *she, Thalia* was the only one in the firing line. "According to the captain, I've simply applied, not signed up yet. He claims when he has my signature on his desk, he'll join us at the next meeting."

"What Thalia isn't telling you is she backed Kel into a corner. As neat as you like." Esther chuckled, obviously enjoying herself.

Heat surged into Thalia's face. "Well he shouldn't make fun of me."

Ty Devereaux burst out laughing, and turned it into a coughing fit. "My hat is off to you, Thalia. I know Kel fairly well and I can't see him sitting around sipping wine and chatting about literary *motifs*. How on earth did you con him into agreeing to that?"

Thalia wasn't proud of losing her temper, but being among friends, people she'd mostly known all her life, fuelled the heat in her cheeks. "He was making fun of our book club without knowing anything about it. When he tossed out some asinine comment about Fifty Shades, I lost it."

Lost it in a cringeworthy way. What was it about the fire captain that drew out the worst in her?

Caroline Joy slapped the arms of her chair and laughed. "Thalia Levonis losing it and telling off Kel Jones—that, I would love to have seen."

"Quite a few Cyprus customers got more than a side of cream with their *baklava* today." Thalia should have worried Mama would hear how her daughter had been rude to a *regular*. She should have been annoyed that she'd lost her self-control. She should have felt any emotion except excitement. And yet, standing up to Kel had been empowering, intoxicating—*liberating.*

"Perhaps it wasn't appropriate in the café, but that man annoys me. As for sipping wine, he can drink arsenic for all I care, but he *will* come to book club when I've joined his crew."

"I'll bring the camera. Such a moment should be recorded." Ty looked at his fiancée and smiled, a stretched-wide, bare-toothed smile that hinted at caveman beneath his urbane veneer. "I like the idea of payback for that kiss Kel gave my fiancée back in March."

Annie patted his knee. "I wasn't your fiancée then and he was being kind and helping me make a certain lawyer realise what he was missing out on. Still, I think we can stir Kel about his taste in literature. How does he even know about Fifty

Shades?"

Esther closed her book, one finger marking her page. "Penny said he buys mainly biographies and travel books from her."

Ty had one arm around Annie's shoulder, his fingers toying with her pearl necklace. "Penny recommended one about Lincoln Hall because she'd sold a copy to Kel and thought it might appeal to me too. But for him to know about Fifty . . ."

Ty shook his head with a pretence of regret. "I fear that Kel's fall from good taste is our fault. It's up to all of us to ensure he makes good on his promise. And Thalia, if you want any help studying the material for your course, I'd be happy to join you. Now I've made the move to Bindarra Creek I feel I should do my bit to contribute to community safety."

"You're going to join the fire brigade too?" Thalia tried to imagine Ty covered in soot like she'd seen Kel earlier this afternoon. Ty in his business suit morphed into Kel stripping off his shirt.

Enough. Theé mou, was she ever going to forget the excitement racing through her body at that sight?

"Seems the right thing to do."

Annie raised her wine glass to Thalia. "Well done, Thalia. It looks like you're building bridges between the physical and the cerebral sides of town."

Esther raised her gin and tonic. There was a clink of ice and a chink of china as book club members raised beer or wine or cups of tea. "Yes, you're on your way to good things, Thalia. Well done."

***

Even the story of survival on Mt Everest wasn't holding Kel's attention. Thalia's flashing eyes and mutinous mouth occupied front and centre of his brain. His mind wasn't interested in cold but in heat. Heat between bodies, the heat of an argument, the heat of holding Thalia.

If he closed his eyes he remembered heat and curves, each curve branded into his skin.

He'd only grabbed her to save her from Connor—and that was a damned lie. He wasn't some white knight rescuing a damsel in distress. Of all the women he knew, Thalia and her acerbic tongue was the least likely to need rescuing. Give her a shield and a spear and she'd run him through.

He hadn't thought of her in that way before. Hadn't thought of her at all, but picking her up had changed things. Inconveniently and irrationally, today he'd seen Thalia as an adult instead of the cute dark-haired child playing at grown-ups when she could barely reach his favourite *baklava* in the display cabinet.

She hasn't grown much taller since those

days.

He'd become aware of lush curves and the sweet honey and spice scent of Greek cooking. Just like that, understanding had clicked into place.

Thali is all woman.

"Kel, where are you?" Dad called from the lounge room.

"On the veranda." He closed his book and set it beside him on Mum's favourite swing seat.

His father carried a mug of coffee in each hand and handed one to Kel.

The dog flap banged, and Maisie's dainty claws ticked across the wood floor. She jumped up beside Kel's father and settled on his lap. In the four years since Kel's mother had passed away, the white poodle had transferred her affection to Dad. Kel came a poor second.

"What's got into you tonight? That light is barely enough to piss by, let alone read a book."

"Yeah, poor choice." He sipped his coffee and grinned. "Nice. You've added rum."

"A man needs something to warm his bones in winter, especially when he doesn't have a woman in his bed."

Only Dad's silhouette showed against the brightly-lit window of the lounge and Kel cursed the low light.

"It's not that cold. Winters aren't as cold as they were when I was a kid."

"Depends how old your bones are. To me, it's cold and lonely and that happens too damn fast. It's time you thought of finding a good woman and settling down."

It had been a while since Dad had raised the subject, long enough for Kel to be surprised now. "Why, Dad, when I've got such excellent company with you and Maisie?"

"I haven't been much company for four years, so don't think you can BS me." He slurped his coffee and hissed. "Damn, that's hot."

"What's brought this on—Mum's anniversary?"

A heavy sigh hung on the cool air.

The familiar clenching in Kel's gut burned like indigestion. Every August since Mum died was the same. Dad spiralled into a depressing sadness. Kel put his own grief aside and struggled to get Dad—to get both of them—through the anniversary. "The florist shop had some of those orchids Mum loved. I thought we could take some when we visit her grave?"

His father shrugged.

A band of iron tightened around Kel's chest.

When had Dad not cared, not planned, not been consumed by their visit to his wife's grave?

"I got a redundancy notice today. The council handed out a stack of them—all of us older workers are being replaced by yadda-yadda-blah technology."

His clenching gut condensed into a ball of lead, heavier than a black hole in space. "Crap. Lousy timing."

The worst possible timing. What would Dad do without work to focus on as they navigated their way through this anniversary?

"Forced retirement is what it is. They call it rationalisation and they've offered a *generous package*, according to the HR hatchet woman."

"Maybe you could take that trip you used to talk about—game parks of Africa through a camera lens, or something like that." Kel knew Africa had nothing to offer his father, that without his job he'd flounder like a tinnie in a storm at sea.

"That was your mother's idea. Why would I want to do that trip without her?"

Kel had used up his annual leave on his last trekking holiday in Nepal. He couldn't take more time off to travel with Dad. Not yet. "Well, what sort of trip would you like to do?"

"Trying to get me out of your hair?"

"No, but I'm concerned about what you'll do with yourself."

"What other retirees do. Nothing."

Nothing?

The finality of the word, the total absence of colour and life and hope, shocked Kel.

Apathy had never been part of his father's

personality. Grief had hacked out his sense of humour and his heart, but this . . . His tone scared Kel more than crossing a yawning ice chasm with only a rope and thin rungs between him and oblivion.

"Join a club, travel, volunteer. Bert Lamarr over at Glenmeer was saying he doesn't know how he'll have time for everything he wants to do when he retires. Maybe you could chat to—"

"Enough. I'm tired. Tomorrow will be soon enough to find out what there is to do in Bindarra Creek when you're over the hill."

"Sixty-five isn't over the hill. The World Health Organisation defines eighteen to sixty-six years as young and—"

"Sixty-five is five years older than your mother got to be. I imagined she and I would be sitting on that swing watching the garden grow right about now. What the hell am I going to do without her?"

Chapter 4

Kel read the same paragraph a dozen times. Nothing sank in. He pushed his chair back from the desk. So much for wrapping up the *administrivia* of the fire station on a Thursday morning. He dropped the paper on his desk and headed to the Cyprus.

The café was empty of customers and he sat in a back booth sipping a Greek coffee made by Thea. Stavros restocked bags of coffee beans behind the counter.

Thalia refilled bowls with packets of sugar. She moved with quick grace, like a gazelle, her movements sure, precise . . . Until she stopped beside his table. She set the thick blue-glass jar down with a clunk and reached for the pottery sugar bowl.

He stared into his coffee, aware she eyed him curiously, quick, covert glances he saw out of the corner of his eye. But as soon as he looked directly at her, her gaze slipped away.

"Good morning, Thali."

She cringed. No bigger than a wisp of frown, a tightening of her hand on the sugar jar. *Not the reaction he got from most women.*

What had he done to earn her disapproval?

Before yesterday, before he'd rescued her, before he'd wrapped an arm around her waist and swung her out of Connor's reach, before he realised he liked her . . . he wouldn't have noticed it.

Today, it scraped over raw emotions. Thalia disliked him.

"Morning, Captain Jones." She made to move on to the booth behind Kel.

Before yesterday, he would never have reached for her wrist. Today, he needed to know why she disliked him.

Today, it mattered.

"Did I do something to upset you?"

A tiny gasp, a small, but noticeable jerk when his hand touched hers, wide eyes and then . . . "You made your opinion of me quite clear when I came to the station."

He frowned. "What do you mean? What opinion of you?"

"You think I'm a nuisance because I—"

"Never. What gave you that idea?" Thalia wasn't a nuisance. *A distraction—definitely—but he wasn't going to complain about that.* For the first time in twelve hours his mind wasn't spinning endlessly around his father's forced retirement, his depression, his grief.

"You told me I wouldn't fit in with your team. I think you want to avoid coming to my book club and you'll find any way to get out of it, even stop me joining the fire service." Her gaze dropped and she drew a quick, audible breath.

He looked down and saw he still held her wrist. Beneath his fingers her pulse sped up and a hint of pink coloured her cheeks.

He released her hand, but held her gaze. "Sorry."

"What for?" She rubbed her wrist as though she'd wipe away his touch.

Did she dislike him that much?

He slumped back against the wall. "Jeez, Thali, take your pick. Whatever you reckon I need to apologise for—picking you up to prevent Connor giving you a dousing, touching you now. But don't accuse me of trying to get out of your book club by foul means. I said I'd come along *when you signed up*. I'm a man of my word."

"Fine. Then go get a copy of—"

He held up the book he'd purchased on his way to the café.

Thalia reached for the book, her eyes wide as she ran a hand over the cover. "You bought it?"

"Man of my word, remember? It sounds interesting. I look forward to discussing the book with you—with your book club."

Thalia at a loss for words was a sight to behold. Whether she'd completed the initial process to join the fire-fighting service or not, he'd go to her book club because he was curious about her. Maybe reading a book she'd chosen would give him a better understanding of this attraction between them. Why she was occupying his thoughts. "You were serious about joining the fire service?"

She blinked and picked up the container of sugar. "Of course. I don't know why it's taken me this long to think of doing it."

"Good, we need people committed to keeping our town safe. If you need help with the course, just ask. I'll be happy to help."

"Help my Thalia with what, Captain Jones?" Stavros appeared beside Thalia and dropped a paternal arm across her shoulders.

A pause followed—a silence resonating with tension and doubt and wide eyes.

Thalia drew an audible breath. "Papa, I've applied to join the fire service."

"The Fire and Rescue, Stavros, the one based here in Bindarra Creek, not the rural brigade." Kel didn't know why it mattered, clarifying which brigade, but it did.

Stavros frowned, the familiar worry lines of a parent confounded by their child. "What for you join the fire department, Thalia? Working in the family café isn't enough for you?"

"That's not why, Papa. It's about contributing to our town. I want to make a difference. I want to feel useful."

Kel heard an echo of his teenage self in her words.

"You are useful—to your mama and to me. This fire service, it will take you away from us."

"No, not away. I'd go to the station only when there was a call to go out, I think . . ." Thalia fumbled and looked at Kel.

"What Thali is trying to say is that we respond to a phone message to come to the station if we can. Thali will still be able to work in the café. Most members work a day job. Not everyone makes it in each time, but that's fine so long as we have four to go out on the appliance."

Stavros looked even more confused. "So you want my Thalia to drop what she's doing here and run to help you put out a fire? On an appliance—what is this? A toaster, a coffee pot?"

"It's what the fire engine is called."

Stavros held up both hands. "Me, I'm still learning the language thirty years after I come to this country." He shook his head and looked directly at Kel. "And why you call my little Thalitsa this not so good short name? Thali—what sort of name is that? You know she hate it, don't you?"

"I didn't know." For the first time, Kel wondered if the shortened name he thought sounded cute actually meant something else in Greek. "I thought it was just a short form. You know how Aussies always shorten names. Mine is really

Kelvin, but nobody has called me that since grade one. I'm sorry if I offended you, Thalia. I won't do it again."

"This is the second promise you have made to me." Her soulful brown gaze met his.

Stavros reached across and patted Kel's shoulder. "Hey, I'm sorry to hear about your dad. That's lousy what they do to him."

Thalia leaned towards him, hands on the table. Concern flickered in her eyes. "What's happened to your father?"

Kel shook his head. "He was retrenched from the council yesterday. Shitty timing—excuse the language, Thali—Thalia."

She waved his apology away. "Why?"

He knew her *why* probably referred to timing, but he didn't want to talk about Mum's anniversary. "Probably because they're making room for younger and cheaper staff. Dad turns sixty-five in a couple of weeks."

Stavros muttered something in Greek and called Thea to join them. A muted conversation between husband and wife in Greek with Thalia interjecting went over Kel's head. Fascinated, he watched Thalia speak. Her hands wove emphasis into whatever she was saying.

She gestured towards Kel.

He sat up straight and tried to curb his impatience. "Hey, this is all Greek to me, but I know Thalia just took my name in vain. What's going on?"

Stavros and Thea nodded to each other and Thalia met Kel's gaze. "Papa and Mama would like to do the catering for your father's combined retirement and birthday party if you would agree."

Kel hadn't thought beyond Dad's helpless apathy last night. He hadn't considered celebrating the forced retirement or marking Dad's sixty-fifth birthday with any type of event. Celebrations and the shell of a man his father had become were incompatible at any time of year, but especially in the month his mother had passed away.

And yet maybe this was an opportunity to mark the occasion and move forward.

"I don't know where to start."

Thalia slid onto the bench seat facing him and set her hands on the table. "Do you trust me?"

With her parents standing at the end of the table, he reined in a snort. "With a hose, not yet. But what do you mean?"

She rolled her eyes and huffed a sigh. "To help you organise your father's party. Depending what night you want to have it, the RSL might have a room available, or the bowls club, and if not, there's the CWA hall. Can you start making a list of guests to be invited, and we'll start planning the menu."

"But I—"

"What's the matter?"

He spread his hands, palms up. "It's too much to ask of you, all of you."

"If it helps to think of it as an exchange of favours—you offering to help me study to get accepted into the fire service, then think of it like that."

Thea's gaze swung between her daughter and Kel. "Fire service? Thalitsa, what are you talking about?"

Thalia pulled a notebook and pencil from the pocket of her apron and set them on the table. "Papa will tell you, Mama. Kel and I have work to do."

"But—"

"Come, *koukla*. We need to leave these young people to plan their party." With dexterity Kel admired, Stavros steered Thea behind the counter and out to the kitchen, all the while apparently agreeing with whatever his wife said.

"Your parents are very kind to offer to cater, and you, Thalia . . . I appreciate your help with this. August is a tough time for Dad and me. Look, as soon as you get your study materials, let me know. You'll be pushing it to complete the first part before next month, but I *am* looking forward to being your guest at the book club, and I want to help."

Thalia looked up and blinked. "Guest, what? Here, take this page and make a start on your guest list."

"You didn't hear a word I said, did you?"

"I'm to let you know when I get the study notes and you'll help me finish the course in time for the book club—yes?"

He chuckled, his day already brighter. "Close enough, Thalitsa."

She reached across the table and touched his hand. Her liquid brown gaze was full of compassion and her pink lips softened into a smile that chased away his doubt and his worry and his ability to think beyond that soft touch. "And we will make this August one to remember—in a good way, yes?"

"Yes." Bending his head, he swallowed a lump of—he didn't know which of the emotions swirling through him it was, but just maybe, it was hope. Feeling happier than when he'd woken, he began making a list.

***

After Kel left, Thalia sat, tapping her pencil on the table in a slow, thoughtful beat. Was it possible she had misjudged Kel? Like most long-term residents of Bindarra Creek, she knew his mother had passed away after a short illness. Alongside her parents and half the town, she had attended Rosalie Jones' funeral, heard the words of love and tributes to a wonderful wife and mother whose life had been cut short.

But the Kel who had sat across from her

today had revealed a different side of himself, one she hadn't expected.

"Thalitsa, darling, are you okay?" Her mother's voice cut into her thoughts.

"I hadn't appreciated how sadness and loss lingers in Kel's life, Mama."

Mama nodded and sat beside her. "How much worse must it be for his father?"

"Maybe I've been mean to him because I didn't understand. Do you think I've been mean, Mama?"

"You don't have a mean bone in your body, but you don't let people walk all over you either. I think Kel needs waking out of his sadness and you're just the person to do it. You challenged him, took him by surprise. Me too. Why didn't you say you were going to join the fire service?"

Thalia bit her lip. Her gaze flicked up to Mama's and away, down to the pencil in her hand. Tap—tap—tap. "It started as a joke almost. Kel stirs me, I respond. He said he'd join my book club when I signed up to the fire service."

Her mother sighed and sat back, arms folded in her lap. "I—see."

"Yes, he's annoying and arrogant—but I think he hides his feelings behind that smug smile."

"He hides his feelings. This is true." An odd note quavered in her voice.

"You agree with me that he's missing his

mother and he's worried about his father?"

"I do. And I think you, my little Thalitsa, are just the person to help him find joy in his life." Mama gave her a quick hug and kissed her forehead. "Now it is time to work. The lunch crowd is starting to arrive."

Thalia turned and surveyed the café, surprised to see it was fifteen minutes before noon. Where had the time gone?

##

A reply to her email requesting an application form and an attached package of study notes was sitting in the inbox when Thalia logged on late in the afternoon. "I've got it, Mama. The fire department has answered my email."

Mama put an arm around her shoulder and watched as she downloaded the attachments and began filling in the application form. If she was quick she could get it back to the department before the close of business.

You'll be pushing to complete it in a month—Kel's words spurred her on.

Once she'd pressed send, she opened the first attachment, her fingers trembling with excitement and with nerves. Breathing deeply, she exhaled a long slow breath and began reading.

Chapter 5

Kel sat at the table with his father, a plate of steak and two vegetables in front of them for the third time in a week. His father seemed unaware he'd repeated the standard meal on each of his turns to cook. When had they slipped into such boring predictability?

"Pass the pepper, son."

His taste for steak disappeared as he passed the wooden pepper mill to his father. "Dad, how about we eat out tomorrow night?"

"Why? Are you trying to get out of your turn or don't you like the steak I cook anymore?"

"It's fine, but maybe we could have variety occasionally?"

"I haven't noticed you cooking anything fancier than sausages or chops. What's going on?"

Kel set his cutlery down and pushed his plate back. "I'm just realising that we've let ourselves sink into routine. We're stagnating here, Dad. It's time we shook things up—starting with our meals. My night to cook so my treat tomorrow. We'll eat at the pub."

His father looked at his plate and slowly nodded his head. "I cooked this last time it was my turn, didn't I?"

"And the time before that. It's no big deal, Dad."

"We're on a merry-go-round—going nowhere. This bloody retrenchment might be the wake-up call I needed. It's forcing change on me whether I'm ready or not."

"Sometimes change can be good. Remember when—"

Kel's pager beeped. He checked the message and tossed his serviette on the table. "I've got to go to work, Dad."

"Want me to put your dinner in the fridge? You'll be hungry when you get home."

"Good idea. Thanks."

"Night, son."

"Night, Dad." Kel lifted his jacket off the peg by the door, grabbed his keys and strode out to his ute. As he drove to the station, he replayed the conversation with his father. In its unpredictability, work never changed and therein lay a conundrum. Until Thalia had marched into his station and demanded an application form, nothing in his world had ever changed.

Now, ready or not, change was coming. And it wore the face and form of Thalia.

By the time the crew reached the town oval

beside the school the maintenance shed was blazing fiercely. Residents who lived nearby passed buckets along a line. Gemma Hayden, whose house sat beside the oval, aimed her garden hose at the nearest rear corner of the shed. The water pressure was poor and her aim, erratic.

Lou backed the appliance into position. Kel kept onlookers out of the way. "Lou, park it there," he yelled over the din and pointed where he wanted her to go.

He jogged across to his near neighbour. "Thanks, Mrs Hayden. We'll take it from here. Water down your house in case sparks fly."

"Will do, Kel."

"And stay behind the fence." He watched to ensure the dressing-gowned figure retreated to her yard.

The crew worked like a well-oiled machine. Dodge took out the hose. Gabe was in place waiting to attach it to the spigot. Kel and Lou herded onlookers and those who'd been fighting the fire out of the danger zone.

Kel watched black smoke pour from the building. The hairs on the back of his neck prickled and when they prickled, he paid attention.

Something felt off. Chemicals stored in the shed would account for the colour of the smoke, but . . .

"Everybody back another twenty metres."

He yelled and waved his arms, moving those on his right along Gemma Hayden's fence towards Wilgara Avenue.

Lou reacted, herding the crowd on her left closer to the grandstand.

Kel returned to the truck. Acrid smoke seeped into his lungs, stung his eyes. He closed the face plate on his helmet.

Crackling, roaring, dancing demonically, the fire engulfed the shed.

"Ready." Dodge braced, aiming the hose at the growing flames.

Gabe opened the spigot and called, "Water on."

Water sputtered from the nozzle, quickly dying to a drip. "Shit—why isn't it gushing?"

An expectant hush settled over the crowd and all eyes turned to the shed.

A small side window blew out with a crack and pop. Flames, fed by the rush of oxygen, reached for the sky. Two small explosions—chemicals, probably—were swallowed in the roar of the fire.

Kel wasted no time. "Dodge, we've got no mains water. Close the nozzle. I'm gonna connect to the appliance."

Figuring out why the town water wasn't flowing would have to wait.

Gabe turned off the spigot, disconnected the hose and attached it to the truck's supply. He called over his shoulder, "Ready—"

For the second time Dodge replied, "Ready".

"Water on."

Aluminium panels buckled as the heat intensified. Two more muted explosions echoed within the burning shed.

Slowly, the water won over the fire and the flames died down.

Once the fire was out and the crowd had dispersed, Gabe and Dodge rolled up the hose and repacked the appliance.

Kel drew Lou aside. "Anything about this strike you as odd?"

The former senior sergeant of police pinned him with a narrow-eyed gaze. "You're the one with all the experience, but yes, there are one or two things that seem odd about this. How did the fire start in the shed in the first place?"

Kel rubbed his thumb across his lower lip. "The window on the far side had been smashed before we got here. Not much glass on the ground outside. And there's the *unlucky coincidence* of the mains water being unavailable."

"You suspect arson?"

"It's likely. Possibly kids mucking around. The ambos noticed an increase in confrontations between a couple of groups and the grandstand is a meeting point for at least one mob of kids. Worth keeping in mind and informally passing the information to your former colleagues."

##

Just before lunch the following day, Dodge knocked on Kel's office door at the station. In one hand he held several pages covered in print and in the other, his water bottle. "I've got the list of items stored in the shed. Last night's fire destroyed the building, but I got the latest stocktake list from the council office."

"Thanks, Dodge. Looks like you got better co-operation than I did." He put his glasses on, took the pages and scanned them, looking for the list of chemicals.

Dodge set his water bottle on the desk and dropped onto the spare chair. He linked his hands behind his head and set one ankle across the other knee, ready for a discussion. "Any information on why the mains line wasn't working?"

Kel huffed out a breath filled with frustration. "The switch had been turned off outside Gemma Hayden's house. The oval and everything east of that was cut off. But it's not the fact it happened that worries me as much as how it happened."

"Weird. Has the council got an explanation?"

"What do you think? Everyone passed the buck." Kel heaved another sigh and rubbed his forehead. Dealing with bureaucracy often gave him a headache. "Trying to get an answer from anyone at Town Hall is like fighting some ancient, many-headed Greek monster. Each time you think you've pinned down a reason, another department requires a reference number to release information and on it goes."

Dodge reached for his water bottle and drank a mouthful. He wiped his mouth on the back of one hand. "What's with you and ancient Greek myths?"

"I didn't say anything about—"

"You did."

Kel shrugged. "Must have read something that got stuck in my head."

More likely it came out of that strange feeling he'd had about Thalia on the way to the call-out; the sense that change was in the air.

Dodge yawned, tipped his head back and read the clock upside down. "Don't know about you, but I'm still tired after last night."

"Trouble sleeping?"

Dodge grinned. "Tessa didn't like having our evening plans interrupted and Tilly woke us several times."

Kel held up a hand. "Say no more."

"Bet you slept like a baby."

"Not so great." He reached for the mug of tepid coffee and swallowed the dregs. "Did you hear about Dad being made redundant?"

Dodge's chair legs thumped on the floor as he leaned forward "Hell, no. How old is he?"

"He'll be sixty-five in a couple of weeks. Trouble is, he hadn't planned on retiring. He's at a loose end, and it's Mum's anniversary just after his birthday."

"Hit the trifecta there, poor bugger."

Kel nodded. "Thea and Stavros offered to cater for his birthday cum retirement party on the twenty-sixth. Thalia's helping plan it. Will you and Tessa come?"

"Sure—I'll check with my better half, but we should be free. Is there anything else you need before I go?"

"No, I'm good. Thanks for getting the list for me."

"Okay. See you Friday at the pub?"

"Yeah. Wouldn't miss the monthly darts challenge. It's about time we showed the other teams who the top players in Bindarra are."

Kel went back to writing his report, including the lack of assistance from council about the water problem, and pressed the save button. His stomach rumbled and he looked at the clock.

Way past lunch time.

Closing the computer, he set off down the street to the Cyprus Café, wondering what the Friday lunch special might be. With any luck, Thea would still have a serve left.

With any luck, Thalia will be behind the counter.

***

Thalia moved the remaining dessert slices to the front of their trays in the display cabinet and closed the doors. She counted the serves of *moussaka* left in the *bain-marie.*

Five! Where is everyone today?

Usually she enjoyed being in charge of the café, but today, the lunch service had been slow. "Looks like dinner tonight will be leftovers." She covered the remaining *moussaka* with foil and slid the cabinet door closed. Had Nico heard her? The kitchen was suspiciously quiet.

"Hi Thalia. What's up?"

She looked up into Kel's smiling face. "Nothing's up. Why?"

"You were talking to yourself and frowning as though the cabinet had offended you."

She glanced at the inanimate piece of equipment and shrugged. "Mama and Papa have gone into Armidale looking for a new fridge for the café kitchen and it's been a quiet day."

"Those two facts don't have anything to do with each other if that's what you were thinking."

"It wasn't." She paused, considering how to broach the topic of studying with Kel. She was well and truly over her teenage infatuation with the good-looking fire captain.

She was, so why, when she thought about spending time with him, did her insides feel like they were on a rollercoaster?

"I was wondering—"

Kel's "In that case—" overlapped her question.

"You first, Thalia."

"No, after you, Captain Jones." She didn't want to see him miss out on lunch again because she held him up chatting about study.

One eyebrow rose at her formality, but he nodded. "I know it's late but does a slow day mean you still have a serve of your mother's special of the day?"

"We do. How hungry are you?"

"Ravenous, why?"

Thalia lifted the foil off the tray of *moussaka* and reached for a plate. "Given how late it is, would you like two-for-one?"

"What's this? Are you buttering up the fire captain before asking a favour?" His crinkly-eyed grin tripped her guilt switch.

"I wasn't—I wouldn't do that." Heat blazed in her cheeks. "How could you think I would—"

Kel held up both hands. "Relax, Thalia, I'm stirring you. Yes please and thank you. I'd enjoy an extra serve of Thea's cooking. I'd also appreciate your company if you can spare a few minutes now."

Thalia looked around the café. Only one table was still occupied inside and the street beyond the windows was quiet. "I'll get Nico to mind the counter if he's still here." She poked her head around the swing door into the kitchen and looked for her younger brother before returning to Kel.

"He's gone. Never mind. I can keep an eye on the counter while you talk." She moved the bell closer to the front of the counter and set the sign, 'If register is unattended, ring the bell' behind it. Not that anyone would need to ring the bell because she would never leave the café unattended.

Kel was seated in the booth he always sat in, tucking into his lunch. He ate with concentration and considerable enjoyment, if his murmurs of appreciation were anything to go by.

As Thalia slipped in opposite him, she realised he'd switched sides, leaving her with a clear view of the café and the counter. It was a small thing of itself, so why did his thoughtfulness make her smile? Shaking her head, she leaned her arms on the table. "What is it you want to talk about—your father's party?"

"That too, but I wondered if you'd got your study materials yet? Barring a call-out, I've got some free time tonight after dinner."

How could asking him be this easy?

"I got them. I was going to ask if you meant

what you said when you offered to help."

"Always, Thalia. I mean what I say." He looked down at his plate. Half of one serve had already disappeared. He swallowed a mouthful and grinned. "This is wonderful. Your mum's a great cook."

Pride spiked within Thalia and she sat up straighter. "My mother is a fine cook, but what you're eating now—I cooked."

Kel looked at his food and then met Thalia's gaze. "Thalia, marry me!"

For one amazing, awestruck moment, Thalia's girlish fantasy reared its head before the woman she was now folded her arms and sat back. "What a wonderful offer. Get a lot of takers with that, do you?"

He chuckled and cut off another piece of *moussaka* with his fork. "Never asked anyone before, but this is seriously good, Thali—sorry, Thalia."

"I accept you mean that as a compliment and I'll ignore your proposal in the same spirit it was given."

"Wise woman." He reached for the glass of water he requested with every meal before picking up his knife and fork. "I love the variety of your lunch specials. Dad's cooked the same meal for his last three turns at dinner. Lunches here in the Cyprus are the only food keeping me going." The flicker of a frown appeared above his nose. He turned his attention to the plate and divided the remaining serve of *moussaka* into quarters.

Perplexed by the conflicting emotions crossing his face, Thalia leaned forward. "Does your father not know how to cook properly?"

Kel's expression hardened in the blink of an eye. His gaze shuttered and a forbidding frown emphasised the 'don't go there' message loud and clear.

She'd never seen him appear so dark and closed off.

"He can cook. He just doesn't care much about food. About anything." The bitter comment was tagged on, as though it had slipped out in spite of Kel's tight rein on his emotions.

Thalia had a fleeting impression of regret flashing across his face before he looked away and scooped more food onto his fork. She blinked. Had she seen what she thought she'd seen? Kel was always charming and joking and teasing people. But that brief glimpse hinted at pain and vulnerability, at depths of feeling she'd never associated with the fire captain.

In that moment he'd revealed a great deal about his relationship with his father. He was worried and unsure how to help.

Kel Jones wasn't just an arrogant pain with an inflated idea of his own appeal.

That version of Kel she could repel with ease.

But the man sitting across the table from her, the man who cared and tried to hide it behind a laughing facade—that Kel was a different proposition. She'd asked and he'd offered to help her study. Starting tonight.

Which version of Kel was she going to be working with? Did it matter now she had glimpsed the man behind the charmer? Now she knew there was more to him than his playboy exterior?

Whichever version of Kel sat beside her tonight, she was in trouble.

Chapter 6

Kel slipped his glasses on and moved his chair close to Thalia's. Her head was bent over her study notes and she traced a finger over the labelled image of an appliance. A faint whiff of cinnamon and honey clung to her hair and the desk lamp revealed a blue-black sheen that made Kel think of a bird's glossy plumage.

"I think I've got the general idea, but there are so many compartments. How do you keep track of everything?"

"Experience. You quickly become familiar with storage of hoses etcetera because we use them most of the time, but items that are only used from time to time need an occasional refresher. On training days, I challenge my team to find a number of less frequently used items in less than a minute. Winner gets shouted dinner by the rest of us."

Thalia tucked her hair behind her ear and turned the page. Blank white paper greeted them. "That's the end of the first lesson. Wow, that's more than enough for one evening. I've taken up lots of your time."

"It's no problem. I consider time spent with you as an investment in my team. You're a quick study."

Thalia ducked her head and picked up her bag, setting it on the table on top of her study notes. "Mama insisted I memorise each recipe as she taught me to cook. Papa taught me memory techniques. Between them, they taught me to take in and retain large quantities of useful information." She reached into the bag and lifted out a square box and set it on top of the bag.

When she lifted the lid the scent of heaven emanated from the box.

Kel leaned forward. "You brought *baklava*!"

"Freshly made this afternoon. I couldn't arrive empty-handed. This is not the Greek way."

Kel's father poked his head around the corner and tapped lightly on the wall. "Mind if I ferret around in here? I can't find the book I was reading."

Kel stood and pointed to the open box in front of Thalia. "It's okay, Dad. We've just finished going through the first lot of notes, and Thalia's brought dessert to share. I'll get some plates."

He walked past his father and into the kitchen, appreciating the positives of the open plan renovation when he glanced back. His father had taken a seat beside Thalia and she was holding the box out to him.

He peered at the contents. "That looks and smells delicious. How do you start making something like that?"

"*Baklava* takes a bit of time and care, Mr Jones, but other Greek dishes are easy enough to make. Do you like Greek cooking?"

"I guess so." His father shrugged and smiled at Thalia, but then, she drew that reaction from most people who thought she was sweet and kind. She was polite to everyone—except him. He knew how whip-smart she was, but him, she treated to her snarky side.

Did he tease her more than others? Had he hit a sore spot with her?

The puzzle of why Thalia treated him differently had never bothered him. It didn't exactly bother him now, but he was curious. *What had he done to earn her dislike?*

Kel shook his head and carried three plates and forks into the dining-study area and set them on the dining table.

Thalia lifted the box from the desk and gently put it beside the plates.

"I guarantee you'll love Thalia's cooking, Dad. And this," he lifted out a piece and handed the plate to his father with a fork, "is what heaven tastes like."

"Big promise there, son."

Both he and Thalia watched Dad cut off a piece and raise it to his mouth.

Kel's mouth watered, but he wouldn't break

into the moment by serving himself and Thalia yet. "Well?"

His father closed his eyes and held up one finger. "Ssh, don't interrupt." He chewed, swallowed, and slowly opened his eyes. Setting the fork on his plate he leaned back in his chair and looked at Thalia. "I don't think I've tasted a dessert as good as this since my wife made her carrot cake recipe and convinced me vegetables in a cake were a good idea."

Thalia beamed at him. "You are very kind, Mr Jones. Maybe I will try making this carrot cake one day."

"Okay, enough talk. Thalia and I need some of her cooking too." Kel served two more portions, offering one to Thalia before retreating to an armchair with his. Quiet munching filled the room for the next couple of minutes, but Kel's mind kept coming back to Thalia's inexplicable antagonism towards him. He didn't want to be the only person she didn't smile at. Thalia's smiles were like . . . like her cooking. He wanted more of both, but they would have to be earned.

"I've had an idea, Thalia. How about we go down to the station now and see how much you can remember about the appliance and the equipment?"

Thalia finished eating and set her plate on the desk. "Like the challenge you set your team? That would be great."

She looked up at him and the overhead light fell on her face. Her lips were glossy and full, and Kel had a sudden urge to discover if they tasted of honey.

Honey and cinnamon and . . .

Once the idea of kissing Thalia occurred to him, it was as though he'd always known he had to kiss her.

But Dad's sitting there eating his second piece of baklava. And I just suggested going some place we'd be alone. His gaze lingered on her lips.

Thalia glanced at her watch, a delicate band of white and yellow gold that looked old enough, she might have inherited it from a grandmother. "Oh, but it's almost ten o'clock. If I'm not home shortly, Papa will be anxious."

"That sounds—" Kel stopped short. Calling Stavros old-fashioned was unlikely to endear him to Thalia.

A glitter that he took as warning flashed in her eyes. Yes, Thalia was no fool. She knew precisely what he'd almost blurted out. "Like a typical Greek father, yes. But I would love to call into the station tomorrow and check out the appliance, if that's convenient?"

Disappointment curled through Kel's belly that it wasn't happening now. Kissing Thalia would have been easy if they were at the station, alone. And a personal tour of the appliance would cement tonight's lesson in Thalia's mind. A personal tour of the station—alone, together, at night—might lead to kisses. It wasn't happening tonight.

But anticipation could be a positive.

"Sure. Locating items without the pressure of needing them will help when you go on your first call-out." Firmly putting aside the desire to kiss her, Kel collected the plates and forks and carried them into the kitchen and dumped them in the sink.

Thalia collected her laptop and stuffed her notes into her shoulder bag. When she had pulled on her coat, she held out a hand to his father. "Goodnight, Mr Jones."

"Goodnight, Thalia. Come for another visit soon, won't you."

Her gaze flicked up to Kel, as though she was uncertain how to answer. "I'll bring you some more Greek dessert if you like."

Kel chuckled to himself. *Neatly side stepped, Thalia.*

He saw her to the front gate, thought about kissing her there and then. "See you tomorrow, and thanks for the *baklava*." He began to lean towards her.

She held out a hand. "Thanks for all your help. I'll see you tomorrow at the station. Goodnight, Kel."

Certain she had divined his intention, he leaned on the gatepost watching as she walked down the street, and waited until she turned the corner. Her lips wouldn't be honey-glossed tomorrow, but he'd still want to kiss her.

He suspected that one kiss wouldn't be enough.

***

Thalia walked home from Kel's house clutching her laptop and bag close to her chest. The cold wind whipped fallen leaves around her ankles, and slipped inside her leather jacket. Quickening her pace, she tried to outwalk the winter chill, but she couldn't outwalk the memory of Kel's gaze dropping to her mouth. Nor could she misunderstand his intention as they stood by his gate. Hungry was the first word that sprang to mind, and not for her cooking.

At twenty-eight, she knew what that sort of look meant, but she'd never expected to see it in Kel's eyes. *Not for her.*

How does a woman resist that look?

Thalia stopped at her front gate. Her cheeks would give away her inner turmoil. Lights in the lounge room meant Papa or Mama or both were still awake, and Nico's car wasn't parked in front of the garage. He was still out enjoying himself, while she had used a mythical time limit to get out of spending more time with Kel.

Why? Because that looked like desire in his

eyes? Anóiti gynakia. And for good measure, she told herself the same in English. *Foolish woman.*

She opened the gate and cringed when it squeaked as she closed it. Tiptoeing up the brick path, she stopped at the bottom of the front stairs and slipped off her shoes before she climbed, careful to step over the creaky third board.

Why on earth was she creeping in as though she'd done something wrong? What use was it if her parents . . .

As she reached for the handle the door opened and Papa stood in the doorway. "Ah good, you're home." He turned and called over his shoulder. "Thalitsa is home."

Mama emerged from the kitchen with a tray of steaming mugs. "Perfect timing. I told your father you'd be home at ten. See, do I know my daughter or what?"

He waved a hand, brushing away her comments. "Yeah, yeah, you know your daughter. I know my daughter, but I know young men too, and that Captain Jones, he looks at you with *the look*. You know the one I mean, Thea *mou*?"

Mama set the tray on the coffee table and sat in her armchair. "The look you gave me the first night we went on a date. My father warned me about it, and told me I was a foolish girl if I let you steal a kiss."

Papa stood his ground and folded his arms.

"That's the one. *That look*. He's a good man but I know what that look means and I've got to make sure he doesn't hurt my little Thalitsa."

Her parents turned their gazes on her and Thalia wished for the ground to open up and swallow her. At this moment, she'd willingly trade places with Persephone and hide in the underworld to avoid this conversation. *This very embarrassing and surprisingly accurate assessment by her parents.*

"Well, did he kiss you?" Mama never held back from demanding personal details.

Acknowledging her parents' combined attack had defeated her, Thalia set down her laptop and bag, shrugged off her coat and dropped onto the sofa. "No, Mama, he didn't, and Papa, Mr Jones was there the whole time so you have no reason to worry about me."

Papa rubbed his hands together and dropped into his armchair. He reached for his mug of cocoa. "I told you we had nothing to worry about, Thea *mou.*"

Mama rolled her eyes, and picked up her mug, but the look she gave Thalia was speculative. Mama would accept she had been given the truth, but she always knew when there was more to a story than she'd been told.

"I took some *baklava* over to say thank you to Kel for tutoring me. His father really enjoyed it.

77

He mentioned it was as good as a carrot cake his wife used to make. I thought I'd try making one for him." Thalia sipped her cocoa. Distracting Mama was only ever a temporary measure.

Mama sat forward and set her mug on the table. "This carrot cake he talks about, it has actual carrots in it?"

"Yes. He said his wife convinced him vegetables in a cake were a good idea. Do you know the recipe, Mama?"

"I know of one version, but the one Keegan mentioned might be a special family recipe. It is always good to have the right recipe when a man you are interested in—" Mama's gaze flicked between Papa and Thalia. "Your Papa fell in love with my cooking."

Oblivious to his womenfolk, Papa beamed at Thalia. "Your mother, she cooks just like my mother used to."

"That is the secret, Thalitsa. Forget fighting fires to get his attention. Give him food like his mother cooked."

Thalia groaned and pushed to her feet. Kel's *marry me* had been no more than an expression of his enjoyment of her cooking, but Mama would turn it into a real proposal if she knew. "I'm going to bed. *Kalinychta.*"

Dóxa to theó they hadn't had this conversation in the café.

And they didn't know she was going to the station tomorrow. With luck and a little help from Nico, they wouldn't find out.

Chapter 7

Thalia hadn't turned up.

Kel finished the last of his paperwork with a sigh. He couldn't find another legitimate reason to stay at the station. On days like this he wished his job were permanent. Then he could remain at the station on the off-chance Thalia came by instead of going back to his building work.

Disappointment weighed heavy on his mind as he drove home. A change of clothes, an early lunch, and he had a new chicken coop to make for Jon Johnson's children next to the family flower farm.

He took off his boots and set them beside the back door. Movement in the kitchen caught his eye and when he took hold of the handle, the back door was unlocked. He opened it quietly and stepped inside. Dad stood at the bench, his back turned to the door.

"Dad, what are you doing home in the middle of the day?" A jumbled pile of paper lay in front of his father and in his hand was an old school exercise book covered in purple contact.

"It was bugging me after Thalia left last night and today, as I was twiddling my thumbs at work because—well, why assign a new case to someone who's leaving?—I remembered where your mother kept her recipe book." He raised the book in question. "Thalia seemed interested in Rosalie's carrot cake. I thought I might drop the recipe in to her at the café."

"That's a great idea. Have you eaten?"

"Not yet."

"Why don't we have lunch at the Cyprus and you can give it to her then?" As well as getting an excellent lunch, he would find out why Thalia had stood him up.

Geez, better not phrase it so it sounds like we had a date.

"Maybe. I was thinking about photocopying the page at work first. Rosalie wrote her recipes out longhand. I—don't want anything to happen to her book."

Dad set the book on the bench, his hand resting over the neat handwriting. A spatter of grease stains fanned across the lower half of one page.

"I reckon Thalia will be really interested in Mum's recipe. And pleased that you thought to give it to her." He glanced at the clock. "How about I go order for us both and you swing by the office and photocopy it now?"

Dad nodded. "I know she doesn't look anything like your mother, but in some ways, she reminds me of Rosalie." He breathed in and out slowly and nodded. "Right. I'll meet you at the café. And can you order me some of that *baklava*?"

##

The Cyprus was busy, even for a Wednesday, but its usual hum was missing. Kel joined the queue at the counter, which in itself was interesting. The Levonis family ran the café so no one waited long for service, but Thalia appeared to be alone behind the counter.

She rang up an order and then moved along the *bain-marie* to serve it. *Where were her parents, and Nico?*

One place ahead of Kel in the queue, Ty turned and spotted him. "Not quite the quick lunch we'd planned."

"Hey, Ty, what's going on with the Levonises?"

Ty glanced towards Thalia before answering in a low voice. "Nico didn't come home last night. Stavros and Thea have gone out looking for him. They've informed the police he's missing."

Kel's gaze returned to Thalia, determinedly holding the fort for her parents. He didn't think Nico was the type to disappear unless something had happened. "Any news?"

Ty shook his head. "No, they went out early to start searching and haven't returned. It's not looking good."

Thalia's usual sunshiny smile was notable

by its absence as she turned to her next customer. He thought he caught a shimmer of moisture in her eyes.

The man ahead of Kel, a stranger in town, looked at his watch and mumbled something about being out of time. He tutted as he left the line and walked out of the café.

Two more groups joined the queue behind Kel, but his father hadn't arrived. Despite the patience of the Cyprus regulars, Thalia was struggling to keep up.

Kel slipped out of the line and waited until Thalia completed an order before leaning close. "Thalia, I can give you a hand if you like?"

She sucked in a quick breath, blinked rapidly and nodded. "Thanks. You can wash your hands in the sink beside the back door. There's a spare apron hanging on a hook beside the sink."

He prepared quickly and came back to stand beside her. "Tell me the orders and I can plate them up."

She held out a register print out. "I'll clip the orders to that railing as they come in. Take them from the right and work your way back towards me. When an order is picked up, put the slip on the spike next to the servery. Here's the first order: two lasagnes with salad. The lasagne is marked where to cut so the servings are uniform. Tongs are hanging beside the salad bowl." She turned to the next customer, her customer-friendly smile a shade less broad than usual. "What would you like?"

Kel set to work. As Annie came to collect her meal, she grinned approvingly. "Good on you, Kel. I should have thought of offering to help."

He shrugged and set two plates on the counter. "I didn't realise I was going to until I had."

Ty picked up two sets of wrapped cutlery from the box on the servery. "Mate, I never thought to see the day you'd willingly put on an apron."

Kel laughed. "Then you haven't been to one of my famous barbecues. Soon as the weather warms up, I'll have both of you and Annie's mother over."

The smell of freshly cooked dishes teased his nose as he plated up meal after meal at Thalia's order. Between them and the efficient set up behind the counter, they managed to make inroads into the queue, and the line rapidly shortened.

Thalia called out the next order. "One *moussaka* with salad, and two slices of *baklava*. It's for your father, Kel."

He'd forgotten about their lunch plans in the rush to help Thalia, but now Dad was here, alone. A sliver of regret hooked into Kel. He didn't like missing the chance to sit with his father, especially knowing the reason he'd come to the Cyprus today.

When his father came to claim his order, Kel handed over the dinner plate. "Hey, Dad, sorry about—"

"Not a problem, son. Glad to see you helping that little girl. I just heard the police are looking for her brother."

"Yeah. And her parents are out looking for him too."

Thalia appeared at his side. "Kel, that *moussaka* won't serve itself." She handed a plate with two pieces of *baklava* to Kel's father. "I think you're getting a taste for Greek cooking, Mr Jones."

"I think you're right, Thalia. I know you're busy, but I have something for you." He set his plate and cutlery on the stainless-steel counter and reached into the inside pocket of his suit coat. "Don't bother looking at it now. It's just a recipe—for carrot cake."

Thalia took the envelope, her lips parting as she stared at it. "I—thank you, Mr Jones."

"Call me Keegan, and my pleasure." He nodded, picked up his meal and moved away from the counter.

Thalia turned the envelope over several times before sitting it beneath a polished stone paperweight on the shelf beside the kitchen door. She tucked a strand of hair behind her ear. "That was very kind of your father, Kel. I will make this carrot cake for him soon." She moved back to the register and they continued to work as a team although it was clear to Kel that here in the Cyprus, in Thalia's domain, she was the one in charge.

And he was fine with taking orders from her . . .

He chuckled to himself. *He'd happily take orders from Thalia under other, more intimate circumstances too. If he ever got the chance, he'd take it.*

***

Thalia looked around the café. Two tables were finishing late lunches as she flipped the closed sign over and shut the front door early. Her neck muscles ached and a headache that had begun hours earlier, when her parents asked if she knew where her brother had gone, flared into full-blown life. She took her phone from her apron pocket and looked for a message.

Any message to end the waiting and uncertainty.

"Anything from your parents?" Kel handed her a mug of coffee, strong and black and absolutely what she needed.

"No." She dropped the phone into her pocket and led the way to a booth in the back corner, choosing the seat facing the front door. Closing her eyes she sipped her coffee.

When she opened them Kel was watching her over the top of his mug. The only other time he'd looked so intently at her had been last night.

Then, his gaze held a different intent, one that had sent her scurrying home like a startled mouse. "Waiting to hear is agony."

"Can I get you something to eat? You look like you've been on your feet for hours."

She shook her head. "Since six this morning. I don't think I can eat, but thanks for the coffee. And thanks for helping. That was very kind." She wrapped both hands around the mug and sipped her coffee.

If Kel hadn't stepped up to help when he had, I don't think I'd have coped.

She blinked and met his gaze. "Oh! You came in for lunch and haven't eaten. Let me get you a plate . . ."

"I'm a big boy; I can help myself. You stay there. Are you sure you don't want something, a samosa—something small?"

She shook her head.

"There's a piece of lasagne left, but not much else. I'll leave the money by the register."

"Don't you dare. I should be paying you casual rates for your help today."

Kel held up both hands. "I'm glad I decided to drop in for lunch today, and I was happy to help. Back in a minute."

Wearing a Cyprus apron with a smear of tomato just above the ties at his waist, Kel shouldn't have looked so good. Thalia didn't think even her good-looking brother rocked the look as well as Kel, despite the number of adolescent and young women who miraculously appeared at the Cyprus on days Nico was rostered on the register.

Nico . . . She rubbed the spot over her heart. What if something truly terrible had happened to him?

A warm hand tipped her face up. "Hey, don't imagine the worst, Thalia. And please don't cry."

"I wasn't."

Kel's thumb brushed away a tear. "Right, you're not crying. This is just exhaustion caused by stress."

Thalia scrubbed at both cheeks. She dragged in a breath that shuddered past her tight throat. "He will be found and he'll be all right. He has to be all right."

Kel took her hand where it lay on the table and squeezed gently. His hand was work-rough and callused, but that human warmth and connection— from Kel of all people—comforted her when she'd thought it impossible to find comfort in this day.

"Okay?"

She nodded. "Sit down and eat while it's hot."

He smiled and picked up his fork. "I'm certain this tastes great hot or cold."

Several minutes passed and Kel had almost

finished eating when her phone vibrated. She pulled it from her pocket just as Kel's pager went off.

"I've got to go, there's a car—"

"The police have found him. He's alive."

Chapter 8

Kel's stomach clenched. He couldn't share his message with Thalia, not when joy had replaced her anxiety. "That's good." He tugged the apron ties and pulled the garment over his head. "I've got to go. That was work. See you later."

She gripped his wrist. "Thanks so much for what you did today, Kel. I really appreciated your help—and your company."

He nodded, not trusting himself to speak, and walked quickly out of the café. What was usually a short, pleasant drive from the café to the station felt interminable. Knowing what to expect made it worse.

He thought about the request for *the jaws of life*—the pager details were sparse, but any time the combi tool was mentioned, the situation was bad. He drove to the station, relieved to find Dodge and Gabe already there. Dodge opened the station doors and looked down the street. "I can see Roman Taylor's car. He's finished the first phase of training so we've got our crew."

Kel sat on a chair, pulling on his work boots. "No good. This is a hazmat situation. We need a fully trained member. Anyone know if Lou is around?"

Gabe leaned on the doorjamb. "She and Warren are in Lake Macquarie for a few days with the twins. Connor will probably be here soon. I saw him maybe an hour ago. He said Eva gave him a list of things a mile long to do in town."

Dodge looked up and down the street. "I think that's Connor's ute turning the corner."

Roman beat Connor through the door and Kel shook his head. "Thanks for responding, mate, but this one you can't do yet."

"Hazmat?" Roman looked disappointed. "No worries. Is there anything I can do from this end?"

"Man the radio. Pretty sure it's Nico Levonis' car they've found."

Silence heavy with knowledge and concern settled over the crew as they climbed into the appliance. One of the town's own needed their help.

Lights and sirens on, Dodge drove the truck the long way out of town, heading north before the narrow link road to the west. "How long d'you reckon the bridge will be out?"

"Couple of months, minimum. Time's like this, you notice the difference it makes." Kel settled back in his seat.

No one spoke.

A few kilometres along Mt Ingalls Road, a police car was parked on the verge, red and blue lights rippling across the top bar. Senior Constable Abby Taylor signalled them and Dodge pulled in behind the police car. A short distance ahead, Constable Agwe Donaldson, the rookie police officer everyone in town simply called AJ, was setting out orange traffic cones between a hazard warning sign two hundred metres down the road and the police vehicle.

Kel was first out of the appliance. He joined Abby and they walked towards the embankment. "What have we got?"

"Nico Levonis. Truckie spotted skid marks and then the tip of his car, stopped to see if anyone was inside, and called it in. There's fuel leaking—petrol, not diesel—and we can't get him out. The car is wedged between two small trees."

Kel nodded and turned to his crew. "Dodge and I will inspect the situation. Connor, Gabe, get the foam ready and start setting up the work area."

The immediate area was clear of power lines, which ran along the opposite side of the road, but when they scrambled up the slope, the smell of petrol was strong.

Nico's small electric-blue sedan was wedged between two medium-sized trees, tilted slightly downhill towards the fence enclosing a dam. The windscreen was opaque with cracks, but the difficulty was the badly crumpled body of the car. Abby had called it right when she'd said they'd need the combi tool.

"I'll get Gabe onto spraying the foam, then see what I can do to stop the leak in the tank." Dodge slithered back down the slope to the appliance.

Kel moved quickly but cautiously around the car, checking for other hazards before he approached the driver's side door. Through the window, he could see Nico slumped against the wheel. If there was an airbag, it had failed to deploy. Blood oozed from a head wound and several streaks ran down the side window.

Kel knocked on the window. "Nico, can you hear me?" A faint groan was music to his ears.

Dodge and Gabe appeared at the top of the embankment carrying the canister of foam and a pair of wooden chocks. Kel moved away from the vehicle before Gabe began spraying the fuel-soaked ground around the car. "Nico's alive. Get Connor onto stopping the leak and call it in, will you, Dodge?"

"Sure." Dodge moved a short distance away and relayed the information to the comms centre. "Comms, one car MVA down embankment and wedged between two trees. Protection line being set up. One person trapped. Request paramedics for male, approximate age twenty-five years, severe injuries and barely conscious. Police are on scene already."

The crackling reply reassured Kel.

Gabe turned off the nozzle. The car sat in the middle of a foamy sea like a Christmas ornament. A somewhat dented ornament to be sure, but now they could begin stabilising the vehicle.

The driver's side was a little higher, angled up where it had come to rest against the bigger of the two trees. The passenger door was inaccessible, even if they trimmed back the bushy branches on the other side of the car. "We'll have to get him out through the driver's side. Connor, grab chocks for the rear and I'll do the front."

Gabe and Dodge attached a rope to the rear tow-point and anchored it. The crew worked with a synchronicity that came from repeated drills and familiarity with one another.

So far, so good, but the more difficult part of the rescue was still to come. Kel needed to focus. He pushed the image of Thalia's joyful expression when she'd learned her brother was alive to the back of his mind.

"Handbrake next. Who's the smallest?" Gabe looked around the group.

They were similar in height and Dodge was at least one shirt-size smaller than Kel. But if anything went wrong, he was the one Kel wanted standing by with a charged thirty-eight millimetre hose. "Much of a muchness. I'll do it."

Besides, rescuing Thalia's brother was

personal in a way Kel hadn't foreseen. Connor and Gabe removed the rear window with a pop, while Dodge donned the BA set and prepared the hose against the slim chance the car ignited.

Kel considered how best to enter the vehicle. There wasn't much room between the back and front seats, or between the crumpled roof and the seats. He slid across the boot, head-first. Gripping the rear passenger headrest, he dragged his upper body through the narrow space until both hands found purchase on the front headrest. The stink of urine and blood assaulted his nostrils and he focused on breathing through his mouth for the next couple of breaths.

His feet hung out through the rear window as he reached a hand between the bucket seats and applied the handbrake. "Brake on," he called, before wriggling onto the back seat. His booted feet barely fitted sideways between the front and back seats. Moving like a circus contortionist he reached down the side of the front passenger seat. When his fingers finally touched a lever, he lowered the seat back and clambered into the space next to Nico. He hauled his mini pack onto his lap, opened it and took out a pair of surgical gloves. Now at last he could make an assessment of the young man's injuries.

"Nico, can you hear me?" The head wound had bled profusely, soaking into his shirt and singlet and matting his hair with dried blood.

How many hours has the poor bugger been stuck out here?

"Water." Nico's voice was scratchy and weak with pain.

"Here you go, mate. Just a small sip for now." He offered a bottle of water.

Nico reached for the bottle and groaned. His right hand fell back into his lap. "Everything hurts so bad."

"I'll hold the bottle. Here." He positioned the straw in front of Nico's mouth.

Nico managed a couple of sips before his head sagged against the headrest. "Ta."

Safety, comfort, assessment—the words were etched in his brain. Kel set the bottle aside. Outside he could hear his crew preparing the combi tool and from a distance, the faint sound of sirens. "Can you tell me where it hurts most?"

"All over."

Kel suspected Nico's left arm was broken, but when he eased forward and looked down, his gut threatened to hurl his lunch. The crumpled front and side of the vehicle explained the bone poking through the flesh of Nico's right leg.

It's not about you; it's about the person relying on you to rescue them. Kel swallowed the bile that rose and continued his assessment.

"Nico, I'm going to lower the back of your

seat and then put a neck brace on you. Don't try to help, just relax as much as you can." Carefully, he manoeuvred the neck brace into position. Next, he covered Nico with a thermal blanket.

Gabe and Connor got to work opening the driver's side. Kel kept up an easy chatter, diverting Nico's attention between bursts of screeching mechanical noise with comments about his family and the café, and touching on where the boy had been last night.

Nico frowned. "Something—something to tell . . . can't remember."

"Don't sweat it, mate. It'll probably come back to you later."

His crew removed the door and Kel sucked in the fresh air that rushed into the vehicle.

Connor returned with the spinal board. As his gaze dropped to Nico's leg, his nostrils flared and his skin paled. He jerked his head to the left and stepped aside. "The paramedics are here."

Kel looked past Nico into the face of the new paramedic in town. Twenty plus years of experience in Sydney if he recalled rightly. Sharon something. Names didn't matter at the moment. "We need the spinal board. Nico has head injuries, and a protruding bone on his lower right leg. I couldn't reach to stabilise it, sorry. Left leg may also be broken, and I suspect his left wrist is too."

Sharon ran an experienced eye over Nico.

"I'll set up a drip and attend to his leg from this side. Are you able to assist with the spinal board from that angle?"

"Yes."

Kel waited while a cannula was inserted in Nico's right arm and the drip set up. Deftly, Sharon immobilised each leg, and passed a sling around his neck to cradle the left arm. Between them, they manoeuvred the spinal board into position and adjusted the straps.

The paramedic signalled her partner to bring the stretcher closer. "Okay, who's helping lift him out?"

As one man, Kel's crew moved in and Kel braced himself against the passenger side door. "On my count, one, two, lift." Despite their care, the boy groaned and passed out.

Probably for the best.

Kel hauled himself out through the driver's side, easing out the kinks in his back as Nico was stretchered out.

"Good work, Kel." Dodge lowered the hose and removed his helmet.

"He's alive, but he won't be dancing or romancing for a while."

"What do you think? Do we stick around until the tow truck arrives?"

"Yeah. At least I got to eat lunch before this call-out."

Abby joined them, and they stood on top of the embankment watching as the ambulance left. Connor and Gabe had begun packing up the work area. Down the road, AJ was keeping an eye on traffic along the Mt Ingalls Road.

Dodge indicated the rookie officer. "AJ's fitting in well."

"Sure is. The Bindarra Creek police force has a grand total of three officers now." Sunlight streamed past the clouds that had darkened the morning and Abby slipped on a pair of sunglasses.

"He got lucky scoring his home town for his first posting." The ambulance disappeared around a bend in the road and Kel led the way down the slope.

Abby jogged the last few steps and came up beside Kel. "If you guys are going to wait for the tow truck, can I get your opinion on something odd?"

"Sure. What are we looking at?"

"Up this way." Abby led them a couple of hundred metres down the road, walking some distance beside a set of heavy black skid marks. "These tyre marks indicate a vehicle that was heading towards Bindarra Creek swerved and lost control."

"Kangaroo? If it was Nico, he might have been tired and slow to react." Dodge looked from the marks to Kel and frowned.

Kel shook his head. "If you're asking for an opinion on these marks, it isn't my area of expertise, Abby. Dodge is your man."

"I'd like both your takes on the scene, but I want to give you a complete picture. Okay, so it's a single vehicle accident and this stretch of road isn't exactly difficult to navigate, but there are also these other tracks." Abby pointed to a set of heavy black marks heading in the other direction. "Once we'd examined both sets—and you have to admit it's unusual to find two sets like this, starting at almost the same spot and going in opposite directions—AJ and I backtracked into the bushes. A vehicle was parked in here and took off in a hurry. The tracks in the dirt are fresh."

Kel and Dodge followed the curving tyre tracks to where they ended, or started. Dodge squatted and pointed to twin lines of deep ruts. "Somebody took off in a hurry. Look at the gravel spray. Question is, were these made by Nico or by someone else?"

He followed the tracks a short distance and squatted again, pointing at a cross weave of tyres. "Look here. I'd say two different vehicles were here, one after another."

Abby added a note in her notebook. "So now maybe the question is, if one of these sets of tracks was made by Nico's car, was he here before, or after the other vehicle?"

"The drivers could have been here together." Kel looked around. Something, some element about the situation niggled in his mind.

Were the tracks left by Nico? "There's a substantial fuel load here. Abby, do you mind if we have a bit of a look around?"

"I was hoping you would offer. I've got this gut feeling that you boys might spot something I'm not seeing." Abby's radio crackled and AJ requested her presence. "I'm coming." She turned back to Dodge and Kel. "Let me know if you see anything, and feel free to tell me if I'm chasing ghosts, guys."

Kel took one side of the short track and Dodge, the other. Slowly and methodically, they searched for a clue that might explain the presence and hasty departure of two vehicles.

"It could have been an arranged meeting." Dodge's voice was thoughtful and incisive, revealing his police-brain in action.

Once a police officer, always a police officer.

"Then again, it might not have been Nico here. We can't assume either set of tracks belong to him."

"Do you believe in coincidence?" Kel didn't and he doubted the former policeman did either.

"No, but some people have the bad luck to be in the wrong place at the wrong time. Look at that." Dodge pointed past Kel's head and carefully stepped across the tyre tracks.

Kel stepped around a bushy, low-growing tree that separated him from whatever Dodge was pointing at.

Ten metres inside a three-strand wire fence stood a hay-shed. Scorch marks ran up not-quite-straight wooden supports. Hay bales were stacked in the central area, and the charred remains of others lay scattered in the dirt beyond the roof of the shed.

Nico's *something to tell* buzzed in Kel's mind. *What if Nico saw something last night and panicked?*

"Kel, over here." Dodge bent down and carefully parted a clump of long, dry grass on the highway side of the fence.

Lying on its side was an empty oilcan. The same brand they used in their drip torches.

"Better tell Abby we need to set up an exclusion zone and then let the investigation unit know. We may have an arsonist in the area."

Chapter 9

Thalia woke with a start. A regular metallic squeaking sound faded as she sat up and rubbed her hands over her face. White sheets, pale walls, an astringent smell of hospital-strength cleaner . . . memory roared back.

These first hours after surgery are critical. The doctor's words struck her as fatalistic, and she'd refused to leave Nico's side. Rubbing her hands up and down her arms, she leaned closer.

"Nico?"

Her little brother lay in the hospital bed, doped up on pain-killers and out for the count. Scooting her chair back from his bedside, she stood, wincing as cramped muscles protested before she picked up his hand. "Nico, can you hear me?"

She watched for any fluttering of his eyes. Nothing.

She pressed her cheek against his hand. It was still and cool. One hand and his face–they were the only parts of her brother not hidden beneath bandages and casts on both legs and his left arm. A body brace enveloped his torso.

Beneath the olive skin that was part of his appeal to the girls of Bindarra Creek, he was pale.

Black and violent-purple bruises rimmed eyes similar to hers. They remained closed.

Thalia walked to the window and peeked around the end of the curtains. The new-minted gold of early morning limned the hills on the horizon. She rubbed her eyes before checking the time on her phone. It was barely six thirty, far too early to call anyone. She dropped the phone beside Nico's water jug.

What time would the doctor make his visit?

Around midnight she had finally persuaded Papa and Mama to go home to sleep with a promise to call them when she knew more. Glancing at Nico, a surge of love for her little brother welled within her. With a single light finger, she stroked his cheek. "I'll be right back, Nico. You know I need my coffee to start the day right."

Tiptoeing might be silly when Nico was doped up, but she couldn't help herself. Holding the heavy door handle down, she closed the door as quietly as she could and went in search of coffee.

By the time she rummaged in her bag and found sufficient change for the vending machine, the buzzing hum of a floor polisher approached and nurses' shoes squeaked past on the tiles.

She opened the door to Nico's room and stopped dead. Kel Jones stood at the foot of the bed. "What are you doing here?"

"Came to see how Nico's doing. The nurses

told me you stayed beside his bed all night. You must be exhausted."

The word alone was enough for her body to feel the pull of gravity, for her gritty eyes to ache. "A bit." She closed the door behind her.

"Has he woken while I was gone?" She hated the need rasping like a file in her voice, need that grated on her taut nerves at Kel's sympathetic "No". The armchair beckoned, vinyl covering, wooden arms and all. She tossed the blue hospital blanket onto the floor and sank into the chair.

"I guess you're waiting for the doctors to do their rounds?" Kel crossed to the window and lifted the curtain. Light spilled around the edge of the drape, reflecting brightly off the stainless steel cabinet beside the bed.

Thalia scrunched her eyes against the glare. "Yes. I promised Papa and Mama I'd let them know when to come in. Is there something you want?" The swish of material and the metallic ting of the curtain puller encouraged her to risk opening her eyes.

For a microsecond—so quick Thalia thought she'd imagined it—Kel's gaze dropped. To her lips? She wasn't sure.

Then he headed towards the door, his expression shuttered like a statue in a cemetery, incapable of allowing emotion to seep through. "I didn't want to disturb you, but will you let me know how he's doing?"

"Of course."

"Thanks." If not for the hint of fresh citrus aftershave lingering on the air, Thalia would have thought she'd imagined him.

##

A few minutes after Kel left, Ishya Bhandari poked her head around the door. Calm and caring, the Nepalese nurse was a favourite with patients and their families. "A—what is it you say—heads up, Thalia. The doctor should be here within half an hour if you want to let your parents know." Her accented English had a calming lilt and her smile was gentle.

"Thanks. Do you need me to leave while you do—whatever you have to do?" Clutching her coffee, Thalia stood. The room spun. She groped for the arm and sank onto the chair.

"Oh, this is not good." Ishya bent over her and a warm hand took Thalia's wrist in a relaxed hold, a nurse's check-the-pulse-without-seeming-to hold. "Besides spending the night at Nico's side, I bet you haven't eaten a thing, have you?"

"I'm fine. I—probably should find something to eat after I ring Mama." Thalia stopped beside Nico, rested her hand on his and leaned close. "I'll be back in a few minutes. Don't you go charming the nurses into a date while I'm gone."

"You go straight to the hospital café. There's plenty of time before the doctor makes her rounds. Off you go." A gentle hand assisted Thalia to the door, urging, guiding, not demanding or pushing, but as encouraging as Ishya's soft words to go and eat.

Blinking away tears—she'd be damned if she let Nico hear her cry—Thalia left the room and followed the signs to the café.

After the quiet beeps and pings in Nico's room, the clatter of cutlery and the buzz of conversation in the small café were like an assault on her ears. She stopped in the doorway. *Was cafeteria food worth putting up with the noise?*

But the aroma of bacon and scrambled eggs hit her nose, setting her stomach gurgling in anticipation. Her last meal had been cereal nearly twenty-four hours ago.

She pushed the brown plastic tray along the metal counter. It slid out of her grip and knocked into the tray of the person ahead of her. Water slopped out of the woman's glass. "Sorry, so sorry." Thalia didn't recognise the customer ahead of her.

"Don't worry, love." The older woman gripped the edges of her tray and turned her ample body, blocking Thalia's path to the register. "My husband's in for an operation. Men's problems, you know, with the waterworks. Got a man of your own?"

"Uh . . ."

"Oh, dear, pretty girl like you should be settled down by now. Why, when I was your age—"

Feeling guilty at cutting the woman short, but desperate to escape, Thalia grabbed the nearest plate of food. Oven-warm croissants with ham and cheese. No waiting around for a server to dish up eggs and bacon. "Got mine. Sorry again about the water."

"Oh, okay." The woman looked disappointed, but as Thalia headed towards the register she heard, "My husband's in for an operation . . ."

She paid and headed towards a table for two tucked into the back corner next to the end window. If she was lucky, no one would disturb her back here. She pulled out her phone and rang her parents.

"Thalitsa, any change?"

"No, Mama. He didn't wake during the night, but Ishya said the doctor would be doing his rounds soon, maybe in fifteen or twenty minutes." Thalia had meant to call as soon as she left Nico, but that head spin had driven thoughts of anything except food from her mind. "I'm sorry it's not much notice."

"Your papa and I are ready anyway. Who could sleep after the night we had?" In a suddenly muted voice, as though Mama had turned the phone into her shoulder, she chivvied Papa to put on his jacket and remember the keys. "We are leaving home now. We'll see you in ten minutes." Mama ended the call in the middle of Papa's protestation he'd been ready since dawn.

The familiar, fond banter between her parents reassured Thalia. If her parents could bicker amicably on their way to the hospital, Nico would recover.

Thalia turned into the hallway in time to see a young female doctor and two police officers enter Nico's room. She hurried to join them, hopeful of learning more about Nico's accident as well as his post-operative condition.

Papa was standing beside Mama at Nico's bedside, his arm around her shoulders while she held Nico's hand between hers. Her parents looked up at her arrival. Tears glittered in their eyes, scrunched-up eyes holding in pain, watery eyes in faces trying to be strong. "Thalitsa, the doctor says they're going to keep Nico in an induced coma to give his brain time to heal."

Thalia glanced at the unfamiliar doctor writing on the clipboard notes. Young, maybe close to her age. Was she qualified to make that decision?

What were the right questions to ask? Thalia's foggy brain knew there were details her family needed, but only one mattered right now. "Will he be okay, Doctor . . . ?" Why didn't all doctors wear name badges like other staff?

"Jess Frobisher. We've done all we can. Now it's up to him; he's young and fit, but for now, we wait." Her voice was pitched low to instil confidence; her tone, reassured, but her suggestion shredded the last of Thalia's reserves of politeness.

"That's it . . . just wait? Who's the doctor in charge? There's got to be more we can do. What about sending him to Armidale or—"

Dr Frobisher might be young, but she quietly took charge of the conversation. "Ms Levonis, moving your brother at this time would be more of a risk. I assure you that the doctor-in-charge concurs with me on that, and on continued monitoring of your brother while we allow him to begin healing."

"But—" Thalia closed her eyes and pressed her lips together. "I'm sorry. I just feel so useless standing here doing nothing."

Dr Frobisher slid the clipboard into its holder and clicked her pen closed. "I do understand, but sometimes the best course of action is to do nothing. Bodies need time to rebuild their defences. Medicine gives them that chance. You're welcome to stay with him as long as you wish. Under the circumstances, I believe hospital policy regarding visiting hours can be relaxed. I'll be back this afternoon if you wish to talk further." Her soft-soled shoes barely made a sound as she left them, shutting the door quietly behind her.

Once the doctor had departed, Abby Taylor tucked her police hat under her arm and pulled out a notebook and pen. "I have some questions I need to ask you—about Nico's movements the night before last. Can we move outside where there are chairs for everyone?"

Mama shook her head and stroked Nico's hand. "I will stay with my son. What can we tell you about that night?"

"What time did he leave home?"

Mama looked at Papa. He shook his head and she turned to Thalia. "I was busy baking for the next day. Thalitsa, do you remember when he went out?"

"Sorry, I left before Nico. I'm studying to become a firefighter and I went to . . . I was studying with a friend."

Abby's gaze met Thalia's. "I didn't know that. Who's the friend?"

Revealing her connection to Kel would be the stuff of total embarrassment. Would the police officer assume they were dating when she knew Kel was tutoring her? "How is that relevant to Nico?"

Mama tutted. "For goodness sake, Thalia. Why you make a fuss." She looked at Abby. "Kel Jones, the captain of the fire service. She went to study with him that night."

The usually unflappable police officer

pinned Thalia with a look that was an odd mix of surprise and something that looked like disquiet.

Thalia wanted to squirm her way right out of the hospital room, until she realised that wouldn't help Nico, or contribute to Abby working out how and when Nico's accident had happened. Rounding up her embarrassment and controlling it like the nuisance it was, she raised her chin and met the officer's gaze. "The captain was kind enough to help me that one time. I'm sorry I don't know when Nico left home. If it's important, one of his friends might know."

Abby nodded. "It would be helpful if you could give me a list of people who might have been with him that night. Any idea where he was going?"

Mama looked thoughtful. "Was there a dance on somewhere? My Nico, he likes to dance."

Thalia pinched the bridge of her nose, trying to catch an elusive memory. Immature in some ways, and a dreamer, her little brother could be easily led. Nico's quiet aside to her in the kitchen that afternoon had worried her, but why? "He was going to swing by a friend's place to pick him up and they were going . . . somewhere. He was talking about a—it might have been a *dare club*?"

As soon as the words left her mouth, the worry returned. "That might not be it, but it sounded like something a schoolkid might do. Nico is twenty-five."

"Dare club? What is this nonsense?" Papa hid behind gruff denial, but she knew; he was hurt she hadn't told him about his own son.

"Papa, I don't remember exactly what he said. As *you* said, foolish things tumble from his mouth at times."

Abby Taylor conferred with AJ, quiet tones from serious faces. AJ nodded and Abby turned to Thalia's parents. "There is talk of a dare club happening out Corella way. Nico's car was found off the Mt Ingalls Road to Corella. We'll check it out."

Papa's expression was a mixture of sadness and the need to defend his son. "This dare club, what do they do?

AJ looked at his superior officer, who nodded, before answering. "It's a group of mostly young men and a few young women who are given challenges to carry out. Most of the tasks are the sort that could be potentially embarrassing if filmed and spread on social media. A few appear to be in the *wild* category. We're not sure if dares earn the person doing the challenge extra points or kudos within the club, but there is usually an element of danger involved."

"It doesn't sound like something my Nico would do. He's a good boy." Thalia heard the fear in Papa's voice, saw it reflected in his eyes, and sweat trickled down her back.

She wrapped her arms around her waist. Was her little brother lying in a coma because something stupid had happened? "It sounds exactly like something Nico could be talked into joining, Papa."

Her gaze flickered over Abby's face. The officer's expression was closed, but she held herself erect—an authority figure who understood good people made bad choices. *Did she believe Nico's accident was the result of a dare gone wrong?*

Thalia couldn't risk asking that, not while Papa was struggling with the idea his little Nico, his son and heir, might have joined such a wild group.

A tear rolled down Mama's cheek. She raised her free hand and wiped it away before stroking Nico's cheek. "He is a good boy, our Nico. He wouldn't do these silly things."

"Mrs Levonis, we need to check any and all possibilities and cross them off our list, even if they seem farfetched. To that end, we'd like your permission to take Nico's fingerprints."

Papa's face took on an alarming reddish hue. "Why you want our son's prints? He's no criminal. He was the one injured in the car crash."

Abby's tone gentled. "Mr Levonis, we need to be able to exclude his prints from the scene so we can see who else may have been there."

"You don't suspect him of anything?"

The hesitation in answering was no more

than a single heartbeat, but suddenly Thalia knew. They were talking about more than Nico's car. Her stomach clenched and she couldn't push a single word past her dry throat. *What aren't they saying about the accident?*

"As I said, we need to be able to exclude Nico's prints from any found at the scene. Do we have your permission, as Nico's parent, to do so now?"

Mama nudged Papa. "Go on, Stavros. Tell them to go ahead so they can find how this terrible thing happened to our son."

Her parents shared a moment of silent communication before Papa turned to the police. "Do what you have to do, but find out why our son is now lying here. If someone caused this to happen, I swear I'll—"

Abby raised a hand, her expression stern. "We will do all in our power to find the truth of your son's accident."

The scanning of Nico's fingerprints was quick, digital and efficient, not like the old television cop shows' black powder on white paper. When they were finished, Abby settled her hat on her head. "Thank you for your assistance." With a nod to Thalia's parents, the senior constable opened the door and stood waiting for her junior constable.

Twisting his cap between his large, capable hands, AJ stepped up to Stavros and thrust a hand out to shake. "Nico's a good bloke. I'll come visit when he's awake again. Maybe I'll stand a chance of beating him at darts if he's on crutches." AJ smiled before following Abby out.

When he's awake . . .

The mention of darts and socialising and the absolute certainty in AJ's optimism touched something deep inside Thalia. She drew in a long slow breath and exhaled it even more slowly, imagining her worries and fears sliding away along the squeaky-clean hospital floor, and out through the dust-coated windows, carried away in the wind whipping up grit and flinging it at the glass.

Nico would wake up . . . because he had a future and friends and a family who would be devastated without him.

Thalia prayed it would be so.

Chapter 10

Kel settled into an uncomfortable plastic chair in the police interview room. High on two walls, radiant bar heaters glowed, red strips promising warmth, failing to deliver. He shivered, unable to get rid of a prickle of unease tensing his neck muscles.

What was so all-fire important that Abby had called him in for an interview about a routine car accident?

Abby and AJ entered and sat opposite him. AJ dropped a folder on the desk and turned to the recording device.

Abby clasped her hands on the desk. "Thanks for coming in today, Kel. We have a few questions you may be able to help us with. Okay if we record the interview?"

Kel nodded, unable to shift the early-morning memory of Nico, comatose and still in the hospital bed, and Thalia's pale face and shadowed eyes. Both images were seared into his tired brain. But maybe his being here would help Abby to find answers about Nico's accident. "Fine with me."

"Good. Now the usual warnings—" Once Abby finished the formal introduction, and recorded details of time, place and those present, AJ slid a folder across. Abby opened it, removed a photo of the accident scene, and turned it to face Kel. "Is this the vehicle accident you attended on—"

"Yes."

Abby's left eyebrow rose, her only reaction in an otherwise neutral expression. "Can you let me finish before you answer questions, Captain Jones?"

Her use of his professional title snapped his attention back to the fact he was in a formal interview. He wasn't talking to his friend, Abby, but to one of Bindarra's police officers. He sat straighter in his chair. "Sorry, Senior Constable Taylor. Go on."

"And following the extraction of the victim and departure of the ambulance, were you and your team member, Dylan Myers, asked by the attending police to assist in searching a section of the verge near the beginning of a set of skid marks? I refer you to the marking on the map and this second photo marked 2-B."

AJ passed both items to Kel.

He put on his glasses and studied the map, checked the photo, and nodded. "That would be the general area we searched." Feeling he'd now got a handle on the reason for, and direction of Abby's questions, he pushed his glasses on top of his head and met her gaze. Abby's actions in requesting his and Dodge's help around the site of the shed fire weren't standard procedure and while they were probably incidental to the inquiry, she had to cover all possibilities.

"Did you find anything out of place during your search?"

"There were tyre tracks and gravel spray indicating a vehicle had left in a hurry. In long grass, Dylan Myers found an empty oilcan. It's the same product we use in drip torches when we back burn, good for starting small fires along a front. Not far from where the can was located, we found a scorched hayshed and bales scattered outside, like someone had tried to put out a fire without equipment."

"I'll come back to that later." Abby glanced at her notes and paused. She pressed her lips together and pinned him with a strange look before asking her next question. "When did you and Thalia Levonis begin a relationship?"

The question hit him like a speed bump taken at speed, jolting him from the path he thought he was on. "Relationship? Where did you get that harebrained idea? We aren't in a *relationship*. And what the hell has Thalia got to do with her brother's accident?" His brain bounced from Thalia to Nico, from relationship to accident. Other than the fact they'd found an oilcan and a partially burnt shed near the site of the accident, what possible link did Abby imagine existed between Nico's accident and Kel and Thalia studying together? "I helped her study one night."

Across the table, there was an audible intake of breath, and a scrape as the table shifted slightly.

Abby turned to AJ.

The young constable was staring at his clenched hands. A muscle jumped in his cheek and his jaw thrust forward.

"Let's take a break. Interview suspended at nine-oh-five AM."

As soon as the red light went off, Abby closed her folder and turned to her partner. "AJ, would you make coffee for us please?" Then she rested her arms on the table and leaned forwards, waiting until the constable had closed the door behind him.

"Did you think the oilcan had been there for long? And yes, I'll ask these questions again with the tape running."

"No. It was new, no rust, and there was a legible price sticker on it." Both he and Dodge had agreed on those details and not touched the can, leaving it for the police to bag as possible evidence.

"So you'd agree it was dropped very recently. We reckon when your fire incident report comes in, it will show that shed fire happened the same night as Nico's accident."

"Coincidence, that's all. He's not done anything suspicious, has he?"

Abby's expression remained police-neutral,

but a flicker of emotion—too quick for Kel to catch a specific nuance—crossed her face. "Why is it difficult to think Nico Levonis might be an arsonist?"

Kel's stomach took a dive as the implication of Abby's line of questioning hit him. No wonder AJ was uncomfortable. Hearing your superior officer suggest your good mate might be responsible for setting a couple of fires would be difficult.

"A couple of local fires we suspect of being arson, and an oilcan on the other side of the road from an accident he was involved in. Bit of a stretch connecting him, don't you think?"

"It might be, if we hadn't recently learned he was probably heading to the dare club out Corella way."

"Still coincidence. Doesn't that come under the heading of circumstantial evidence? I know he was coming back on the Mt Ingalls Road from Corella, but that doesn't make him an arsonist, or mean that he'd been to that club."

"True." Her gaze flicked to the door and back to him. "But why would Nico have a drip torch in his boot if he wasn't intending to start a fire?"

"What?" Kel inhaled an audible breath after the single syllable.

Nico—an arsonist?

The two words didn't belong together, and the bizarre idea floated like ash on the wind, refusing to settle. Kel racked his memory.

Had Nico been at the sports shed fire? Was he one of those personality types who got his jollies watching flames, or the flurry of activity?

Geez, poor Thalia and her parents will be devastated if that's true.

Thalia.

Abby wanted to know how Kel's connection to Nico's sister fitted in.

"Look, I have no idea if you're on the right track, but I haven't seen any evidence of intent from Nico. I'm pretty sure he wasn't at the sports oval the night the shed burned down, and he hasn't been at any of our recent call-outs."

AJ returned with three mugs of coffee. He set them in the middle of the table and resumed his seat.

Abby tapped a slow tattoo on the closed folder. "Maybe not. Let's resume recording." She waited until the red light came on and picked up the thread of questioning. "Interview resumed at nine-oh-twelve AM. Can I take you back to my previous question—when did you and Thalia Levonis begin—if not a relationship, then at least what she called a *one-time study session*?"

"The night before Nico's accident was the

only time we've had a study session. I offered to help her with some course content she was unsure about. My father was in the house while she was there. She left just before ten o'clock and walked home."

"Did she say anything about her brother going out that evening?"

"No."

"Did she say she had told her brother that she was coming to your home to work?"

"There was no mention of Nico at all. We focused on her study notes, ate *baklava* with my father, and then she left. That was it. A simple evening of study."

"Have you ever done that sort of study session with other applicants for a position on your team?"

Kel thought about the various crew members who had joined his team since he became the captain. "Aside from chatting over a beer, no, I don't believe I have."

"Why did you make the offer this time?"

The tips of his ears burned, but there was no easy way around saying it, no way for him to quell speculation about his interest in Thalia except by admitting to his foolishness. "It's part of a silly challenge Thalia and I made. I said I'd go to her book club the day she joined the fire service. She rocked up asking for the forms, and she's determined to follow through. I admire her persistence."

Abby's lips gave a slight twitch before she continued with questions she'd asked informally during AJ's absence.

Kel answered, sipping his coffee between questions, unsurprised to discover it had cooled by the time Abby wrapped up the interview.

"I think that's all for the moment. Thanks for your co-operation, Captain Jones."

AJ turned off the recorder, and Abby flipped the folder closed and pushed her chair back. "I'm impressed, Kel, at the lengths you're prepared to go to, to enlist new members."

Kel rubbed the back of his neck and stood. "Shouldn't that be the other way around—the lengths Thalia is prepared to go to get me to her book club?" Despite the moment of levity, he didn't feel light-hearted. Nor did he feel a buzz at the possibility they had found their arsonist. Not when there was a chance that Thalia's brother was the criminal.

Abby chatted about inconsequential things as she walked him out. They stopped inside the front door and she fixed him with a serious gaze. "Kel, one thing—don't mention any of this to Thalia during your study sessions."

"Of course not, but just so we're clear, there is no *relationship* between me and Thalia."

"I hear you, but you need to distance yourself from her for now."

A weight dropped into the pit of Kel's stomach. Abby had nailed it. Distancing himself from Thalia was the right thing—the *sensible* thing—to do. They had no *relationship*, so why did he feel this ridiculous sense of disappointment?

Thalia had been to his home precisely *once*.

He'd held her in his arms precisely *once,* and not in the way of a *relationship.*

So why am I thinking about it now?

He didn't want to think about it, not with Abby's astute gaze cataloguing his every reaction. "Have you lifted Nico's prints off that drip can?"

"You know I can't comment on an ongoing investigation."

Kel opened the door and held it, blocking the entrance with his body. "If Nico's prints are on that drip can, I'll do the shirtless run with '*I heart the police force*' in neon zinc on my back."

"You're that sure? Maybe, Kel, you should think before making rash bets with the women in Bindarra Creek." She winked, a slow, non-sexy, *you're-definitely-crazy* wink he found strangely reassuring.

"Abby, this is one bet I'm confident of winning."

But as he drove to Jon Johnson's place to begin delayed work on the chook house, Kel's mind ticked with details from a course unit he'd taken on the psychology of arsonists, back when he was considering applying to work for the investigation unit. He was still thinking about it three hours later when he flicked the catch on the door of the finished coop and stepped back to look over his work.

Arsonists weren't always disaffected members of the public or pyromaniacs. There had been that firefighter who craved the adulation and hero-worship of being the town saviour so much, he'd set fires so he could put them out. And he'd been caught when it finally dawned on his captain that the firefighter was always first to respond to a call-out.

Geez, was there a pattern Kel was missing? Was there someone on his team who turned up to every fire? Who was first to the station each time?

Usually me. Geez, what a comforting thought.

He needed to thrash through possibilities, but sharing details before he could absolutely dismiss each of his team was problematic.

He hated suspecting anyone; it left him alone, and in a lonely place.

Uncertain who he could trust, he chose to avoid the station. And the Cyprus Café had to be off limits until Nico was brought out of his coma and shared what he'd seen. Until then, Kel couldn't tell

Thalia that Nico had seen something. The investigation was official and he couldn't be seen with her. And they definitely couldn't share any more study sessions.

Feeling like a pariah, Kel called in to the truck stop for a meat pie and carried it across to a picnic table under a sloping corrugated roof. Adding to his discomfort, the wind picked up grit and tossed it into his eyes and his pie. Turning his back on the wind, he munched through the slightly soggy, grit-starred pastry and mourned the loss of Thalia and Thea's Greek specials in the café.

And if Nico was the arsonist, how would she feel seeing the man who helped catch him eating in the Cyprus Café? When would he taste her *baklava* again?

***

Ishya finally persuaded Thalia to go home around one o'clock. "There isn't any more you can do for him now. Go home, rest. I promise I will call you if there is any change. Come back when you've had proper food, a shower and some sleep and talk to him some more."

She knew the nurse spoke sense, but the thought of leaving her little brother shredded her heart. What if something happened while she was gone, while he was alone with no one to get help?

Always she had been the one to keep an eye on her younger brother. Three years younger and the only son of her parents, he had been spoiled and perhaps a little bit pampered. *Like our boy cousins back in Greece.*

But big sister Thalia loved her charming, handsome little brother. She'd face down dragons to keep him safe, including the doctors in the small Bindarra Creek Hospital.

Closing her eyes for a moment, she tried to recapture the positive vibes from AJ. The staff in the hospital were devoted to their patients. Nico would get well. The rational part of her mind knew he was hooked up to monitors that would alert nurses to any change.

But he needs his big sister by his side.

"Thalia? He will be fine." Ishya's cool hand touched her forearm.

She opened her eyes and looked down on Nico's sleeping face. "Do you think that will help him, Ishya? Talking to him when he's in a coma?" Maybe she was grasping at straws, but she needed to do whatever she could to help Nico recover.

"If you are asking for scientific proof, I don't know. But if you are asking what I believe, then yes, I think he will take comfort from your presence. But you must look after yourself if you are going to be fit to look after your brother. Eat, rest, and return this evening."

By the time Thalia returned to the café, Papa and Mama were almost finished with the lunch service. Thalia kissed Papa's cheek and looked around the lunch crowd. "Have you seen Kel today?"

"He hasn't been in. How was Nico when you left?"

"The same, Papa. Ishya told me to come home and sleep."

Papa took hold of her shoulders. A frown formed as he inspected her face. "Thalitsa, you have dark shadows under your eyes. Go and rest."

"Yes, Papa. I'll take a plate of lunch with me too. That croissant this morning in the hospital café wasn't fresh."

"They dare call that junk food they serve a café menu?"

Mama joined them, leaning on the counter. "They don't appreciate food like we make it."

"Thea, have you seen Kel today? Thalia was asking about him."

That tore it.

Her stomach clenched and her throat seized up as Mama's attention zeroed in on her like a bee to a pollen-rich flower.

"Thalitsa, you will never catch the attention of a man like Kel Jones if you look like that. Go—sleep."

A wave of anger rose. She had offered to stay with her brother through the night because she couldn't do otherwise. No one would look their best after a bedside vigil like that.

"I guess a day and a half without sleep isn't good for anyone's looks. Isn't it fortunate then that I don't want to catch his attention? I don't want to catch any man's attention." She slapped a serve of lasagne onto the plate Papa held, took it from his hand and strode away.

Home felt too far away and too much effort once the brief surge of adrenaline dissipated. The bed in the tiny flat attached to the back of the café would do her for now. Later, if she couldn't sleep, she'd go home and shower and try again in her own bed.

And tonight, she'd be back at Nico's side.

Chapter 11

"When can we expect Nico to wake?" Thalia pushed wearily up from the armchair beside Nico. The floor rippled beneath her and the room melted like a Dali painting in muted neutral tones. Gripping the headboard until the edges bit into her fingers, she drew a couple of deep breaths until the doctor came back into focus. Tonight, no matter what, she needed sleep.

Doctor Frobisher's gaze zeroed in on her, as though she knew exactly what was going on in Thalia's cotton-wool head. When Thalia released the headboard, the doctor bent over the observation notes, adding another set of neat initials to match those Thalia had seen after her morning visit, and returned the board to its holder at the end of the bed. "He won't *just wake*, Thalia. We will bring him out of his induced coma when his injuries have had sufficient time to heal."

"Right. So there's no chance of him waking in the night?"

"None." She clicked her pen closed and slipped it into the pocket of her jacket. "You're welcome to stay of course, but I highly recommend you go home and sleep. No one functions well, or makes the best decisions, when they're sleep-deprived, and Nico may need you and your parents to make decisions about his ongoing care in the coming days."

"What about?"

"Whether to move him to a major hospital for further treatment once his injuries have begun to heal. But now is not the time for this discussion. Please consider going home and sleeping." The young doctor smiled, a quick quirk of her mouth that was sincere despite its brevity.

Jess Frobisher had done the early morning rounds, and she was still here at—Thalia checked the time on her watch. Eight-thirty. "You were on duty this morning, weren't you?"

Doctor Frobisher nodded. "Yes. It's been a long day—for both of us. I'm heading home now."

Thalia looked down at Nico and her fingers brushed a curl that he'd never been able to tame into submission. It fell over his forehead just right of centre. "That's a good idea. Will you be here tomorrow morning?"

"Bright and early. Good night, Thalia. Sleep well." The doctor left, quietly closing the door behind her.

Thalia dropped a kiss on Nico's forehead. He hadn't allowed her to kiss him like that since he'd hit his teenage years, when being kissed by his sister had become *uncool*. "You can object to my kisses when you wake up, little brother. I'll be back in the morning and then I'll tell you what I've learned about fires so far, and how to fight them. Night, Nico."

Thalia ambled down the corridor and left the hospital through the side entrance closest to Nico's room. At the driveway entrance, she turned right, following the dirt footpath along Court Road towards the bowling club. Beneath a cold, clear, starry night, a westerly wind tugged hair from her messy bun and whipped it across her eyes and into her mouth. She turned her head and blinked, trying to clear grit from her eyes.

In the past, especially on nights like this, she had borrowed Nico's car when she went out.

Never again.

Nico's car was a write-off, and it was past time she bought a car of her own. Although now she'd thought about walking the Silk Road, why would she need a car? Walking everywhere was good training, although barely adequate by itself. What she needed was a plan. A get-fit plan that would toughen her up for her Silk Road adventure and whatever lay ahead in her Fire and Rescue Service training.

She blinked to clear the last of the grit from her eyes and trudged on. Kel had talked about training sessions, and how he encouraged his crew to work on their weaknesses.

"Everyone has them."

"What's yours, Kel?"

"That would be telling. Never give someone that much power over you." He'd looked sideways at her, all sharp-angled cheekbones and hidden blue depths behind his glasses at odds with the teasing note in his voice.

What was she supposed to make of that look?

Across the vacant lot, Kel's house was visible. A light was on in the front room, and a figure she was sure was Kel passed behind the window.

Why had he shown up at the hospital this morning? She'd been too tired to think of asking, and then he'd gone.

The wind gusted, carrying a stink from the industrial bins at the rear of the Bowling Club. Head down, Thalia hurried towards Main Road and a sealed footpath, holding her breath until the wind subsided.

Cr-a-ack.

The sound of breaking glass stopped her in her tracks.

A screech of metal. A thud.

Curiosity beat caution and Thalia hurried to the rear corner of the car park and parted the leaves of the oleander bush. Dull security lights on the rear corners of the bowling club's main building cast limited light, enough to see a dark-clad figure holding what appeared to be a bottle of wine.

A burglar!

She pulled her phone from her coat pocket. The police station wasn't far. If they hurried, they could catch the thief.

Thumb hovering over the home button, a snick caught her attention—a spark—an orange ribbon climbing hungrily towards the bottle. But that was wrong. Ribbons should fall, not rise.

Thalia edged closer, gripping the rolled metal fence railing. Why was the streamer defying the laws of gravity? What was the thief doing with the wine?

The man's arm carried the bottle behind him, stretched his other arm straight, like a javelin thrower, shuffled a couple of steps forwards. The bottle arced through the air, a splendid, perfectly formed arc, living orange and yellow streamers trailing, a thing of beauty. At the top of the arc, he released his grip. The bottle sailed through the broken window. Shattered, cracked, transforming the dark room into dancing fire demons.

Thalia gasped and covered her mouth with both hands. Her gaze darted to the man. *Had he heard her?*

He took several quick steps backwards and stood watching the fire.

When she'd been studying with Kel, he'd

mentioned arson—the deliberate setting of fire. *Was she seeing an act of arson?*

Backing away, she pressed the home button on her phone.

Nothing happened.

Casting a look towards the bowls club, she dithered. A menacing orange glow grew as she watched. Flame tips flickered above the window ledge. Her phone was dead and challenging an arsonist would be stupid. But just across the vacant block, Kel was home. She was sure of it.

She shoved her phone in her pocket and ran, stumbling across the uneven ground towards the lighted window. Across the road, up the front path and then she was banging on the front door.

The door opened and a veranda light flicked on, blinding her.

"Thalia! What's wrong?" Kel lifted his glasses and set them on top of his head. A book closed around one finger hung from his hand.

She pointed across the vacant lot. "I think I just saw the arsonist . . . the bowls club . . . He lit something and threw it inside." Fear, not exertion, chopped her phrases, broke her breaths into shards as sharp as broken glass.

"Stay here and phone it in. I'll go and look." He set his glasses and book on the hallstand and grabbed a jacket from the coat rack.

"My phone's dead."

"Here, use mine." He grabbed it off the hallstand and passed it to her. "Password is Bindarra's postcode." Then he was off, running back the way she'd come.

She stood on Kel's veranda. Even in the couple of minutes since she'd seen the fire start, it had taken hold, grown, blossomed like an exotic flower.

Thalia's fingers shook as she tapped in the password number, and then pressed triple zero. Behind her, Keegan Jones strode onto the veranda.

"What's all the fuss? What's happ—" He peered at the flames shooting out of the bowls club's windows. "Has Kel gone?"

"Yes." Her call connected and she turned her attention to giving concise details. "Fire service . . . there's a fire at the bowls club on Main Street. Captain Jones is already there."

Following Kel, Thalia crossed the road and the vacant lot and was standing on the opposite footpath before she realised she'd moved. Flames crackled, spilling light that danced like demons over the car park. Flames that sent hot tongues through shattered glass, licking the night air. Flames that revealed no sign of Kel.

"Where is he?" Shoving his phone into her pocket, she darted across the road. A wall of heat repelled her before she got past the gate.

"Kel!" Her shout disappeared in the roar of

greedy fire.

And then . . .

Through the glass of the back door she saw Kel wielding a fire extinguisher. He doused the flames licking the doorway of the burning room and directed the hose inside.

Thalia hopped from one foot to the other, wanting to help, unable to move beyond the heat blasting through the windows. In the distance she heard the wail of sirens along Mt Ingalls Road. *Thank goodness nowhere in town is far from anywhere.*

How could she help? With no training and only the first packet of study notes covered, there was little practical aid she could give.

I could go around the front and direct them into the car park.

She sprinted to the corner in time to see the fire truck turn onto Main Street, lights flashing to the accompanying siren. Waving her arms like an aircraft controller, she indicated for them to go around the back of the building.

The truck pulled up and Lou Myers jumped out.

Thalia ran to her. "Kel's inside. He was using a fire extinguisher."

Lou turned to the burning building and frowned. "Okay, thanks. Stay back here and keep an eye out for the police."

Thalia's eyeballs stung with grit and smoke. Keeping an eye out for anyone other than Kel was a big ask.

Where is he?

Scrunching her eyes she tried to see him through the smoke and the flames and security lights. She took a too-deep breath filled with smoke, and coughed. Eyes watering, sinuses burning, she groped for the fence post and turned her back on the flames.

"Thalia, are you okay?" Keegan Jones put an arm around her shoulders and led her across the road; not far in distance, but the westerly wind blew cleaner there.

Sucking in a breath of less smoky air and with two quick coughs, Thalia nodded. "I'm okay. Hard to breathe." She blinked and wiped her eyes on her sleeve. "Kel was inside. I saw him briefly. He had a fire extinguisher. Shouldn't he have waited for his crew?"

"He would have if he thought he needed to. But if he saw an opportunity to slow the fire and assessed that he could safely do so, he'd have taken it." Keegan folded his arms and turned back to watch the fire. "He's a stickler for safety. You won't have to worry about that when you join the service."

Thalia watched the crew swing into action, trying to imagine herself as part of that team. Lou connected a hose to a hydrant, Dodge held the nozzle, and two others—she couldn't tell who they were beneath their protective gear—worked together like a dance ensemble.

The heat didn't appear to faze them, nor the flames leaping through the window. The heat had repelled Thalia.

How do they front up time after time and fight fires like this?

She bit her lip and wondered where Kel was, where the police were, and what the heck she thought she was doing. *What madness let me think I could do this?*

A piece of corrugated iron roofing buckled in the heat and crashed to the ground. Thalia jumped, sparks flew, and Dodge turned the water onto the leaping flames. Heart thumping, stomach clenching, she felt as though each spark prickled her exposed skin like sparklers, multiplied by a hundred. Fear and doubt stole her breath.

Gradually—a minute, an hour, she had no idea—the flames were beaten.

"They've got it now." Keegan's voice came from beside her.

She'd forgotten his presence as she watched the fire crew in action.

A lone figure appeared, walking along the path at the side of the building. Kel moved to the truck and leaned against it, wiping his hands down his jeans and seemingly content to stay out of the way and observe.

"There's Kel." Relief and lingering smoke made her voice husky. She touched Keegan's arm. "He's okay."

"Never doubted it for a moment."

"How can you be so sure? That fire was intense." Being so close to the blaze was frightening—the sensation of heat burning her skin, sucking every ounce of moisture from her eyes. Watching Kel fighting the flames had frightened her more. Rigid muscles ached as she consciously unclenched her hands.

How could she possibly find the courage time after time to face the fire demons?

Keegan patted her shoulder. "For all that he acts like he hasn't a care in the world, my son is careful, sensible. He'd never do anything to jeopardise his crew, and he respects the element he battles. *Know thy enemy*. Have you heard that saying?"

"Of course. Do you mean he's studied and knows all there is to know about fires?"

"Who can know everything? But he knows a hell of a lot. They'll be a while yet and it's cold out here. Come on home, lass, and I'll make you a hot chocolate."

"Thanks, Mr Jones, but I don't want to be a nuisance."

"Call me Keegan. I may not be much of a cook, but I recommend my hot chocolate will cure your smoky throat quick smart."

"Is Dad trying to sell you on his post-fire cure-all?" Kel stood in front of her, a streak of soot arrowing across one cheek and flecks of black coating his face and body. "If you're not sure, let me tell you it's actually quite good."

Thalia looked from father to son. Identical eyes, identical expressions, almost identical smiles looked back. *Appealing. Safe. Comforting . . . Dangerously tempting.*

Exhausted by her vigil and her fears, walking home alone after the fire couldn't compete. *Not with hot chocolate.*

"Maybe I will take you up on that offer after all. Thanks. And then I'll call Papa to come and pick me up."

Kel shook his head and took her elbow as they picked their way across the vacant lot. "No need to call your dad out. I can drive you home."

"But—"

"No buts. Your quick thinking in alerting me and phoning the crew has saved most of the building. Hot chocolate and a ride home in the fire captain's car is the least I can do to say thanks."

Kel's thanks, and the support of his arm— they had nothing to do with the squiggly feel-good vibes in her stomach. So much attention from the fire captain meant nothing more than the thanks he'd given her.

A job well done, that's all it is. And yet his thanks, his touch, and the appreciation in his gaze, were potent in combination.

"Don't you have to stay and make a report or something?"

"Not my call-out. Lou was in charge; she'll have the pleasure of writing this one up. Tomorrow will be soon enough for me to add my part."

He held the door open for her to precede him into his house and eased her coat from her shoulders. "I'll give this a shake outside. Have a seat."

Keegan followed her inside and kept walking through to the kitchen. "I'll get this hot chocolate happening. Do you like extra sugar in yours, Thalia?"

"No thanks, Mr—Keegan."

She sat back in the old-fashioned armchair, too tired to sit up like a lady, straight-backed like her mother sat when they had guests. Too tired to think now the rush of adrenaline had gone. Just—tired.

***

Kel shook out Thalia's coat and returned to hang it on the hallstand, and to offer a quip. Her eyes were closed, dark lashes swept down over shadows under her eyes. He'd be happy to leave her sleep, but his father dropped a stainless-steel pot. It clanged on the tiles and Thalia's eyes slowly opened.

"Have you slept since yesterday?"

"Yes." Her voice had a smoky-husky *sexy* quality, sexy in a way that made him want to scoop her onto his lap and kiss her until he heard how she sounded whispering his name. How had he never noticed her voice—how had he failed to notice *her*?

He shoved his hands into his pockets and dropped into an armchair across the coffee table from where she sat in his mother's chair. "I'll bet you had a cat-nap this afternoon and then went right back to the hospital to sit with Nico."

"I slept." Her gaze slid away.

Yep, a cat-nap.

Funny how quickly Kel had begun to read Thalia. Maybe it was easy when her guard was down, when she was tired and probably running on emotion and several cups of coffee. "Were you walking home from the hospital when you saw the fire?"

"Yes. There's no change in Nico of course. Doctor Frobisher explained that there won't be any change until they bring Nico out of the induced coma. I—don't think I registered what that meant this morning."

Kel's father joined them, carrying a tray with three steaming mugs and a plate of store-bought biscuits. He set it down on the table and handed a mug to Thalia. "There you go, lass. See if I'm not right about the healing properties of hot chocolate after a fire."

Thalia raised the mug, closed her eyes and inhaled. "Mmm, smells wonderful." She took a sip and then looked at his father. "Tastes heavenly. You're a man of your word."

"Not as good as your *baklava*, but this is one thing I can prepare well." His father sat back on the sofa and sipped from his mug. "As good as it always was if I do say so myself."

"Mr Jones, I wonder if—"

His father raised an eyebrow and tut-tutted. "Are we back to the mister now, Thalia? And after I've made you a *heavenly* drink. I'm disappointed."

Was his father joking? When was the last time Kel had heard humour pass his father's lips? A sense of awe, of wonder and gratitude filled him. Thalia was a one-woman miracle worker with her *baklava* and her gentle, warm personality.

Gentle? Thalia? He all but snorted into his hot chocolate at the notion of those two words in the same sentence and yet . . .

He watched as Thalia grinned, a lovely wide smile that lit her face and chased away the tiredness from her eyes.

"Keegan—sorry. Please tell me if you hate this idea or if I'm being forward, but would you like me to show you how to cook a few easy meals?"

His father's mug hovered just below his chin, and he looked over it at Thalia for several heartbeats. "Greek dishes?"

Fascinated by the change unfurling right before his eyes, Kel peered intently at his father. *Humour and now . . . Was that a spark of interest in his eyes?*

"By all means if that's what you want, but I'm happy to teach you to cook whatever you prefer to eat." She hesitated, and her glance slid over Kel like the soft brush of her hand when she had returned his phone. A hint of pink in her cheeks might have simply been warmth returning to her body. But there was a look in her eyes he'd never seen before, a look as inscrutable as Eve and as lethal to his reason as wildfire to his body.

She turned back to his father, leaving Kel disorientated, as though caught in the middle of heavy smoke. "I could show you how to make some of the dishes your wife used to cook?"

His father sat still, his expression flickering between emotions of doubt and hope, until it settled on—*possibilities*.

There was no other word for the eagerness Kel hadn't seen since before his mother had died.

His mother had been a reasonable cook, preferring cakes and biscuits to meals, and she had brought joy and laughter into the heart of their home with her experimental baking.

Softly so he didn't break the magic of Thalia's offer, Kel set his mug on the table and leaned forwards. "You found Mum's cookbook, Dad. Maybe you could look through that and see if you can find a main meal that isn't steak."

Their gazes connected, held, and then his father burst out laughing. Rusty for being suppressed and unused, still it was the nearest thing to a belly laugh Kel had heard in four long years. Dad's laugh loosened a knot of loss and grief and fear he'd carried inside.

"I'll wager my entire superannuation you told Thalia about my miserable cooking and she's taken pity on me, having such an ungrateful son." He turned to Thalia. "Or are you taking pity on Kel having to eat the same meal every time I cook?"

"Maybe I'm tired of him showing up every Wednesday at the Cyprus and moaning with pleasure as he eats my *moussaka*. It's enough to drive other customers away."

Kel's gaze connected with hers. "You don't want my custom at the café? I can go elsewhere if my *appreciation* of your cooking is too much. Would you prefer that, Thalitsa?"

She kept a straight face . . . for all of five seconds, and then she laughed.

He liked her laughter, open and genuine, and her sense of humour. She'd kept that hidden from him too, offering snark and snipe and sarcasm. What other treasures did she keep from general view? Or was it just from him?

"No, my parents and I, we love your appreciation, and the wonderful recommendations you give anyone who asks. Please don't stay away because I'm joshing you."

"I won't." As if he could stay away from her now . . .

But Abby Taylor had told him to keep his distance while the investigation of Nico's accident was ongoing. Which meant no more study sessions, no more banter in the café, no more contact—

"Kel?" His father's voice broke into the regret coursing through his mind.

"Sorry, what was that, Dad?"

"Do you remember what your mother called that casserole she used to make?" He set his mug on the table and strode to the kitchen and rummaged in a drawer. "Found her notebook. Give me a few minutes to find Rosalie's recipe."

Kel's pleasure in the moment, in the positive vibes zinging between his father and Thalia, was swallowed by the reality of a police investigation.

Into Thalia's brother.

He floundered, searching for an easy topic to keep Thalia talking. It might be a long time before they got the chance to sit and chat again, and if Nico was proven to be the arsonist, would Thalia want to be near him? *Not if she thinks it's my evidence that will put her little brother in jail.*

"Tell me about your mother's cooking style. What did she like to make?"

Grasping at the conversational lifeline, Kel thought for a moment. He'd loved most of the dishes his mother had cooked and tonight, Thalia's offer had reminded him of those good times. Sharing food with his family, chatting about their respective days, that coming together of a close family – these were the things he missed after his mother's death. "Mum used to experiment a bit with meals, so I have no idea if what Dad's looking for will be a proper recipe or not."

"Experimental can be innovative." Thalia wrapped both hands around her mug. "Maybe your mother was a culinary whiz."

"It's hard to remember the actual taste of what she cooked. Mainly what I remember are the good times."

"Meals should be a coming together of family and friends. Lots of memories are made over food, and maybe when your father cooks some of your mother's dishes, the taste will bring pleasant memories rather than sadness and missing her."

Good memories—that's what Kel needed to focus on. If he could do that, and if his father accepted Thalia's offer, maybe they could begin to heal, together.

"Will I have to tell the police what I saw tonight?"

The change of topic threw him until he realised Thalia knew nothing of the police investigation into her brother. That was going to come as a shock. "Yes, but tomorrow is probably soon enough. I can take you to the station if you like?"

Lulled by their chatting about food and Mum, the words slipped out before he thought of the implication, and the senior constable's prohibition on spending time with Thalia. Why couldn't he remember such a simple fact? It had been front and centre of his thoughts mere sentences ago, and yet the invitation to pick her up had slipped out. A natural idea, this wanting her company. It felt right, but it was so wrong.

She didn't know he'd been told to distance himself from her. His gut cramped. How could he get out of it without letting Thalia know that? And when she did, she would hate him for suspecting her brother.

"I can walk there from home, but thanks for the offer."

He should have felt relieved, he should have shut his mouth and thanked his lucky stars Thalia was independent. He should have taken his good luck and run, metaphorically speaking, as far as he could. Instead, disappointment kicked his gut like a fire hose when he wasn't ready for the blast of water, sudden and uncontrolled and demanding his complete attention.

Why, against all that was sane and sensible, did he want Thalia to want to spend time with him?

Thalia set her mug on the table and her tongue touched each corner of her mouth, seeking the last of the hot chocolate. "I wonder when the arsonist left? I imagined after what you said the other night that he'd hang around to watch the fire. Isn't that part of why they start fires—so they can see the response?"

"It's often the reason and usually how they—" Realisation hit Kel like a blast from the fire hose, dousing his regret, washing away his doubt.

Nico is in hospital in a coma. Nico couldn't have started the fire.

He looked at Thalia. Understanding filled him with joy. He jumped to his feet, took her face between his hands and kissed her lips, hard. "Brilliant woman. I've got to talk to the police right now."

The sooner he talked to Abby, the sooner he could begin to talk to Thalia as he wanted to, with soft words and softer kisses, with lips and tongue and hands telling her that he wanted her.

Chapter 12

Kel's phone call to the police station diverted to Senior Constable Abby Taylor—or just 'Abby when I'm at home', she'd said when she opened the door to him. "Looks like Riley and AJ are still in attendance at the bowls club."

Even though it was after ten o'clock and her day off, she invited him in, her pet Chihuahua curled on her arm. "Roman and the boys are camping out in our new tent."

They sat on the stone-coloured corner sofa and Kel shared his revelation.

Abby stopped stroking Pinky and looked at Kel. "A neat theory, but even though Nico Levonis has the ultimate alibi for tonight's fire, we can't eliminate him from our investigation into the hayshed fire. Not—" She paused and narrowed her gaze on him, a look that assessed him, deliberated carefully and came to a decision in the space of two heartbeats. "Not when his fingerprints are on the drip torch found in the boot of his car."

Kel slumped forward, his elbows on his knees. He hadn't expected that piece of damning evidence. "I thought . . . No, of course you're right. Sorry, I wasn't thinking."

"You were hoping against the odds, Kel. It's understandable. But from what you've described, there are several points of difference between the fire in the hayshed, the one at the sports shed and what happened tonight at the bowls club."

Kel let his head thump back against the chair. "Yeah, the delivery method has changed for starters."

He knew what that probably meant, but voicing it defeated him. Voicing it spelled the end of barely begun hopes about Thalia. "Could be a copycat who doesn't know all the details of the earlier fires. I hate the idea of us having to deal with one arsonist let alone thinking we might have a second wannabe out there."

"It chills my blood. How anyone can deliberately set fires to damage buildings or start a major bushfire is beyond me." Pinky whined and jumped off Abby's lap, took a few steps and then looked back at her mistress. "I'll just put Pinky to bed. Won't be a minute."

When she returned, she sat on the edge of the sofa. "I'd like to talk to Thalia Levonis as soon as possible and find out what she saw. Then we'll feed in what we know so far about the three attacks and see if we can get a profile of our crim."

Kel cringed inwardly, but it was better to be up front with Abby. "I offered to bring her into the station tomorrow when I come in. You'll need to talk to both of us."

Impatience flickered across her face, drawing twin frown lines above her nose. He'd expected that, but not the sympathy in her gaze. "I know it's tough, Kel, but remember what I said about distancing yourself? It's as important now as it was before, maybe more so."

"It's okay. She said she'd walk there. I'll come alone. But you're wrong about young Nico, I'm sure of it."

"You can't possibly rule somebody out on pure instinct."

He sat forward, his hands hanging loose between his knees. "Before we rescued him and he passed out he mumbled he had something to tell."

"A confession? That would make our job a whole lot easier. You didn't think to mention this earlier?"

"It slipped my mind. But, Abby, what if he saw something, someone?"

Abby drew a deep breath and exhaled before answering. He liked that about her, that she took the time to consider possibilities. "It would be nice to have Nico hand us the arsonist all wrapped up in a credible witness statement. But Kel," her voice dropped, soft with pity and a certainty he was wrong. "What if Nico *is* the arsonist? You've got to prepare yourself for that outcome."

His lungs constricted around his breath, and

his heart hammered against his ribs like a prisoner seeking release. "So, Nico's prints on the drip torch keep him firmly in the picture for the hayshed fire?"

"Yep. Sorry to burst your bubble."

"Don't apologise for doing your job well." He stood, drained of emotional energy and grateful he'd dropped Thalia home before coming to Abby's. "See you at the station in the morning."

"*Captain*," Abby touched his arm and smiled. "If I remember correctly, and I'm certain I do, you said you'd do the shirtless run with '*I heart the police force*' in neon zinc on your back. I'm looking forward to that."

Digging deep, Kel mustered a smile, probably a pathetic attempt, but Abby accepted it for the effort it was.

"You can paint the sign on my back for me."

***

AJ's tight black curls were bent over the keyboard as Thalia, clutching the strap of her souvenir Greek handbag far too tightly, opened the door of the Bindarra Creek Police station and stepped inside. She'd never set foot in the station before and the pine-scented air surprised her, distracting her from the unease that had plagued her since Papa's questioning over breakfast.

"So you just happened to be near Kel Jones' house and you happened to run to get him. Why were you there, Thalitsa? Why did you go that way home?"

"I was at the hospital, Papa, you know that. And without Nico's car, I have to walk."

"And so you walk and you see this arsonist. Why you not think about calling me to pick you up? Why you not more safety-aware?"

"I am safety-aware, Papa, but Bindarra Creek is a safe town. I can walk anywhere and I see people I know."

"You know this person who set fire to the bowls club?"

"No, Papa, I didn't see his face, but I wasn't in any danger. Besides, I always carry my phone."

She hadn't told him it had been flat. She hadn't told him she was afraid. She hadn't told him that running to Kel's house had been instinctive, that seeing his face, hearing his calm voice, had made her feel all would be well.

She hadn't told him, because that would give Papa ideas, wrong ideas about his daughter's feelings for the fire captain. And Mama—if Mama knew why Thalia had run to Kel's, she'd be planning their wedding within a month.

Thalia shivered at the prospect. But Kel made her feel safe. And after the past week, she was prepared to concede that maybe she had misjudged him all this time. Maybe he wasn't a butterfly when it came to the women of Bindarra.

"Good morning, AJ." She pinned on her

best greet-the-customer smile and met AJ's beautiful brown eyes.

AJ came around his desk and leaned on the counter. "Morning, Thalia. How can I help you?"

"I was the one who rang the fire service and the police last night, about the fire at the bowls club. I think I'm supposed to give a statement to someone?"

"Yes, we'll need you to make a statement, but I can't do it. I'm here alone. Abby or Riley—I mean, Senior Constable Taylor and Senior Sergeant Morgan—should be in around eleven o'clock, or you could come back at tree—ah, three this afternoon?" A small frown flickered across his face as AJ corrected himself.

Thalia loved AJ's Caribbean accent, the way he sometimes dropped the 'h' in a word. And she loved how the Donaldson family had adopted children from different parts of the world, giving them a safe home and bringing the world to Bindarra Creek in their little global family.

"Can't I just give it to you, AJ? I really want to get back to the hospital after work at the café."

"Sorry. I'm still on probation."

"Okay, I'll try to come back this afternoon." She gave him a quick smile and turned to go.

"How's Nico?" An edge of fear, of asking a difficult question, one whose answer he might not like, coloured AJ's voice. Thalia knew he hated asking, but Nico's good mate just had to know.

"He'll be in an induced coma until the swelling in his brain subsides. I sit with him and talk to him about anything and everything. Even what I'm learning about fighting fires. Maybe it doesn't do any good, maybe he doesn't hear me. But maybe, somewhere deep inside, he knows I'm there. If my presence and my talking to him has even the smallest chance of helping Nico, I'll keep doing it."

"Do you think it would be okay if I visited . . . and talked to him?" AJ's question was polite, but one hand curled into a fist, and a muscle twitched in his cheek.

He's Nico's best friend. Nico is important to him too.

Thalia lightly touched AJ's hand on the counter. "That would be wonderful, AJ. Thank you. Anytime you want, please feel free to sit with him."

She turned to go. The front door opened before she reached it, admitting Abby followed by Kel. Thalia's gaze sought Kel's before she remembered why she was here.

"Hi Abby—I mean Senior Constable. I came in to give my statement about last night's fire, but AJ told me he couldn't take it without another officer present. Are you free to hear it now or—" She trailed off, her gaze drawn back to Kel. His blue eyes weren't connecting with hers, and he gripped his Akubra like he needed a barrier between them.

Her heart stuttered, raced, lodged in her throat. Where was the relaxed man of last night?

Abby glanced from her to Kel. "Captain Jones had the same idea. Would you mind coming back later, Ms Levonis?"

Kel's silence combined with the senior constable's formal tone and made it clear Thalia should leave and come back later. "Sure." Awkward without knowing why, Thalia looked down and headed towards the door.

Kel stopped her with a hand on her arm.

Through her jacket, she felt his warmth, remembered how safe the same touch had made her feel last night. Remembered a flicker of warmth that maybe she'd misjudged him. Had she been wrong?

"Thalia, I'm sorry to put you out, but after last night we're on alert. I'm trying to rearrange my building schedule so we have someone manning the fire station at all times."

Of course he is.

The rigid thrust of his jaw, and that damned hat he held with both hands, crushing the brim, shook Thalia out of her self-absorption. The threat of an arsonist running free in his town worried Kel. More and more, she was coming to realise he was a protector, a guardian of Bindarra.

He's like Horatio holding the bridge, she

thought. *All steely-eyed resolve, going in to fight for his town with—a hose.*

The image of Kel, bare-chested, standing in the middle of the bridge over the Akuna River, fire hose at the ready—that was some fantasy.

She smiled up at him, noting the concern in his eyes, hearing the impatient tapping of fingers on the counter. Abby Taylor was keen to have her leave.

"Not a problem. I'll come back later." With a nod to Abby and a smile for AJ and Kel, she left the station.

Something was off. It wasn't just about giving her statement. She could have cut the tension between Kel and Abby with a knife.

Shaking her head—she had more important things to worry about than other people's business—she walked quickly along Willow Tree Drive towards the café. Her parents were trying to keep the Cyprus running while worrying about Nico, and Thalia resolved to fill the rest of the morning with cooking, so that this afternoon, she could give her statement to the police, and then visit Nico.

##

"Here, Thalitsa, afternoon tea." Mama set a tray on the coffee table.

Zeus, Nico's German Shepherd, trotted behind her, dropped and rested his head on Thalia's feet. He whimpered, the sound echoing Thalia's sense of Nico's absence.

She bent down and stroked his head. "You're missing him too, aren't you, boy? I'll take you for a walk later."

Mama sat beside her on the couch and handed her a slice of cake. "Have you spoken to Kel about the retirement party for his father?"

Thalia raised the cake to eye level. Fine orange slivers of carrot patterned the cut side. "Mama, is this the carrot cake recipe Keegan gave us?"

"Keegan? Since when are you on first name terms with him? Is this polite?" Her sharp gaze cut through Thalia's response before she could make it.

"He asked me to call him by his first name last night, after the fire. He made hot chocolate and told me it would cut through the smoke I'd inhaled." She bit into the cake, tasting a wonderful blend of subtle flavours. "Mmm, this is good."

"I needed something to stop me going mad thinking about my son, lying in that hospital bed. Concentrating on a new recipe helps. It is good, isn't it? I think I will add it to our cabinet, if Mr Jones doesn't object." Mama bit into her slice, nodding as she did when she was pleased with something she'd made.

"Do you want me to ask him?"

"When will you see him?"

"I'm going to see Nico after I've given my statement to the police. Maybe I could pop in and see him before I come home." Thalia forked up another piece of cake. Moist, with subtle flavours, and the cream cheese frosting was—

"Will Kel be there too?"

"Probably not. I heard the fire crew are on alert and that Kel is staying at the fire station. They're worried the arson attacks are going to increase."

"Hmm, you go see Mr Jones, and maybe take him a piece of carrot cake. Tell him this one is from me when you take it to him. You will have to make the next one. And drop some in to Kel at the fire station."

"Mama, stop with the matchmaking."

"Who's matchmaking? Not me."

"Right, and you didn't tell Ty Devereaux what to do to catch Annie's interest, or give Angus and Claire McGregor a nudge? Mama, I love you, but please let me live my life how I want to."

"Thalitsa, I let you do all sorts of things I would never have done, but you aren't giving me grandbabies to care for. And Nico, my boy might leave town if he doesn't find what he wants to do here." Mama tucked a strand of hair behind Thalia's ear and sighed. "But me, no, I won't match-make. I don't think you're going to need my help. Not with the way the captain looks at you."

She stood, stacking their plates and picking up mugs. "Just be sure he tastes your cooking. That will make sure he proposes to you." With a nod that showed everything was settled, at least in Mama's mind, she headed to the kitchen, her once quick strides slowed by the slight roll and a drag of her left leg.

Thalia blinked at the image of Mama's imperfect steps, her slower than usual exit a wake-up call. Her mother was slowing down and Thalia had failed to notice the imperceptible changes until now.

Was that how it had been with Kel and his father too? The sudden realisation his father had reached retirement age while the years of mourning Rosalie Jones slipped past in a blur of grief?

Growing older meant so many changes, and ultimately—loss.

Thalia rubbed her hand over her chest, over the spot beneath which her heartbeat thumped with good health, good living, and the sure knowledge that one day, it too would burst with grief.

Zeus rose, stretched, and dropped his head on her lap. Liquid brown eyes looked up at her and he licked her hand.

"You're sad too, aren't you, boy? But Nico *will* come home, I promise."

There were no guarantees in life. Nico's accident was proof of that. But if there were no guarantees, was she a fool to resist getting to know Kel on a different level? Was it foolish not to live in the here and now?

Maybe if she was a little more friendly and a little less prickly, she might find they had more in common than *moussaka* and a love of walking. She might even break through the emotional barrier he'd raised and find the man behind the mask.

With renewed determination to think positive, she pulled on her jacket, picked up Zeus' lead and her shoulder bag, and set off to visit Nico.

Chapter 13

"I can't put my finger on precisely why, but I think our arsonist is getting ready to escalate his activities." Kel looked around the table at those of his crew who had been able to make it to the impromptu lunch meeting at the Royal Hotel.

"Did Abby have more information? You saw her, yesterday, didn't you?" Lou took a sip of coffee and pulled a face. "Ugh, I should have asked for it extra hot."

"It was a formal interview, Lou."

"Your second in less than a week. So? Did she say anything? Does she have any suspects?"

"They've begun profiling what they know and maybe we should do the same from our perspective. But can we leave that for the moment and concentrate on how we deal with this."

Dodge leaned on the table and tapped the top with one insistent digit. "Kel, I've had enough experience with your hunches proving correct to go along with this one. What are you proposing we do?"

"I'd like to go through the roster and double-check we have a full crew available in town at any given time over the coming weeks. That attack on the bowling club was more daring."

Lou nodded. "Mid-evening, soon after the club closed for the night, and not many days since the fire at the oval. I agree. We've got to be more than just ready for another attack."

Kel was grateful he had the insights of two former police officers on his team. Dodge and Lou could be relied on to cut through to what was important. "True, we've got to be quicker responding and set up a watch on whoever is around. Can we manage to have a fifth team member in civvies, arriving separately and noting who's hanging around? See if we can't suss out our arsonist."

Heads nodded around the table and Lou pulled out a notebook and pen. "I'm happy to draw up a roster. We'll take turns being on call as the watcher. Slip in under the radar. Maybe we could enlist our newest recruits? What do you think, Kel? Ask Ty and Roman and Thalia to help out with observation?"

"Roman and Ty maybe. Not Thalia." Nobody else in his crew knew about Nico and the drip torch. And he couldn't tell them, not when Abby had sworn him to secrecy.

Lou's head came up like she scented his BS on the air. And that was the flip-side with having former police officers on his team. He couldn't keep much from either Lou or Dodge. Lou pinned him with a narrow-eyed look and he squirmed in his seat, like a fish on a hook.

"Why not Thalia? She called in the bowls club fire and thought to come out to the road and signal us around the corner. What is it with you and pretty women? She called you out the day she came in to sign up. Is that why?"

Damn, he hated improvising. It was just another way of lying, and it sat heavy with him. But he'd given his word to Abby.

"I'm not petty, Lou. You know me well enough to know I don't hold grudges. But Thalia's too conspicuous. Roman and Ty, they'll blend in better."

"Rubbish." Lou left it at that, but she cast a slant-eyed gaze at him when they stood and the team left the pub.

Lou wasn't going to let him get away with that excuse for long. Could he hold off further questions until they caught the arsonist?

Anyone underestimating the intelligence and persistence of the women of Bindarra had best steer clear of Lou. And Abby . . . And Thalia. If Thalia learned he'd vetoed her participation, and why, he'd have no chance with her until this was over. *And if Nico was guilty?*

He'd have no chance at all.

##

Kel found it easier to think in the quiet of

the fire station. He clicked on Lou's report on the bowling club arson attack and read through her concise summary before opening a blank document and typing a report of his non-official involvement.

Thalia Levonis knocked on my door at approximately eight forty-five p.m. and alerted me to an arson attack on the bowls club.

Thalia.

He'd opened his door to a frightened, breathless, beautiful woman whose hair had been a wild mess. He liked that she'd run to him, that she'd thought of him first. Long into the night, he'd lain in bed imagining pulling off the hair tie holding her hair back and running his fingers through her glossy curls.

The screen went dark, pulling him back to the present, to the report he was writing. He read back over his first sentence and continued.

I gave Ms Levonis my phone to call the fire service after she told me her phone battery was flat and left her to make the call to the emergency services. I proceeded to the fire.

He thought about the flare of awareness, the thrill that ran up his arm and raced through his body when her fingers brushed his. Had he deliberately fumbled taking the phone to prolong their contact? She'd brought her other hand up beneath his, ready to catch the device.

And when she'd offered to teach Dad to

cook . . . What Thalia was doing for his father was nothing short of a miracle. Four long years Dad had been existing in the void left by the death of his wife. Four years of grief and dull, unremitting mourning. Four years of *not living life*.

Thalia's offer had sparked some deep-buried will in Dad to re-engage.

Kel glanced at the time and back at the screen. Dammit, he'd been sitting here for half an hour and what did he have to show for it?

Fifty-eight words.

Dad got the miracle and Kel got distracted. That's what Thalia was doing to him. Stealing his ability to think of anything but her. Abby's prohibition on contact between them wasn't helping. Kel had enough brain cells left to realise that. Determined to finish, he read back over what he'd written and then continued typing.

Her quick action helped limit damage to the structure.

He'd seen the fear in her expression, seen her determination to conquer it and do what needed to be done. And he'd wondered how she'd handle the house on fire scenario in the first training session. Walls of flame, blinding smoke. Deafening. Roaring. Frightening.

The thought of Thalia going into such an inferno tripped every protective instinct he had. She'd call him out for being sexist if she knew, but it felt wrong on every level to think of Thalia—all five feet three of her—heading into a blaze to protect others.

And yes, he acknowledged the irony in accepting Lou and Mandy in the same role. But this was Thalia of the divine *baklava*, Thalia who had stomped her foot and flashed her eyes and challenged him, who had brought interest and joy back into his father's life. How could he bear to deliberately allow her in harm's way?

Focus, dammit. He put his fingers to the keyboard.

I proceeded inside the building and . . .

"Knock, knock. Anyone there?"

A slender, feminine hand gripped the edge of the door and pushed it open before Thalia's dark curls appeared, followed by the rest of her.

Kel pushed his chair back from the desk and stood. "Come in. What can I do for you?" Too late, he attempted to rein in the pleasure in his voice at seeing her. Pleasure that would make it even harder to step away from the attraction he felt each time he saw her, was near her, smelled the scent of honey and cinnamon that surrounded her.

His new favourite scents.

"I went to the hospital, and I've just come from a quick visit to your father."

"At home? He's clocking off right on time since they made him redundant. Fair enough too, I reckon."

"I agree. Yes, he was at your home when I called in. Mama made a carrot cake using your mother's recipe and she wanted him to taste it. And to see if he would mind if we add it to our offerings in the cold cabinet."

From the front of the station came a deep bark and a short series of high-pitched yips.

"Sorry, that's Nico's dog, Zeus. He's tied up out the front. Do you mind if I fill his bowl with water? Won't be a minute." She hurried to the sink and filled a small bowl, which she carried outside.

When she returned, she opened her shoulder bag and held out a plastic container. "I have a slice of cake for you, if you'd like it?"

Kel forced his gaze from contemplation of her rich, dark-chocolate eyes to the box in her hand and chuckled. "That looks more like a quarter of the cake than a slice. Are you trying to fatten me up, Thalia *mou*?"

She tipped her head to one side, and her lips—he almost groaned at the memory of them, glossy with honey—parted. "Where did that *mou* come from?"

He shrugged. "Hmm, I hear your father use it sometimes. What does it mean?"

She stepped closer to the desk, set the box down, set her hands on either side of the box and leaned towards him. A breeze wafted through the open door and there it was, the scent of everything wonderful on her skin, in her hair. The scent of Thalia.

"Be careful how you use a word like that. It carries power and connection and . . ." She drew in a slow breath. "It's an endearment, like *my darling*."

Soft, sultry tones like a lover's fingers through his hair, rippled across his skin, his mind, his desire.

"It means *my Thalia*."

No wonder it rolled off his tongue as though the name belonged between the two of them, connected them. It felt right because it was right.

"A potent word."

They stood without speaking. An age passed, several heartbeats that Kel didn't want to end. Not when Thalia was here with him, away from prying eyes and police prohibitions.

And then she stepped back, away from the desk and away from him. "I should go and let you get on with your work." Was that regret in her voice, or wishful thinking on his part?

He could show her the appliance, put into practice the lesson they'd gone through the other night.

He'd had the same idea the first night they'd studied together. And he'd had another idea, about kissing her in the privacy of the fire station. He reached out, a don't-go-yet plea. "Wait. While you're here, why don't I show you the parts of the appliance?"

"Really? Practical revision would be great, but—are you sure I'm not holding you up from your work? You looked pretty deep into it when I arrived."

"A report on last night's fire. Lou wrote the official one. It won't take me long to finish."

If he could manage more than a sentence without it tripping memories of Thalia.

"Well then, yes please." She set a bag outlined with Greek shapes on his desk beside the box of cake before leading the way out to the appliance.

***

Excitement raced through Thalia as she stood beside Kel. Not the excitement she should have felt at putting her theory into practice. That excitement would be acceptable, understandable even to Papa.

The feeling that shivered through her was different. It had nothing to do with learning, everything to do with the man at her side, with how his attention made her feel special, desirable. Like how she'd imagined it might be before reality and Kel's string of casual romances with everyone but her intruded and robbed her of that dream.

I'm not sure if I've forgiven him. But maybe

I'll enjoy a taste of what it's like to be the centre of his world. Eyes wide open.

For all that she'd told Mama she wasn't interested in the fire captain, she knew herself for a liar. She'd never stopped wanting him to look at her. To see *her*.

She perched on the edge of an old wooden table neatly stacked with equipment. Kel leaned on the table beside her, one hand a hairsbreadth from her thigh. She swore she could feel the heat of his body, even though he didn't touch her. Heat that woke those squiggly feel-good vibes in her stomach and challenged the sedate rate of her heart to sprint.

She faced the appliance and blew out a soft breath.

Kel began, his voice taking on the tones of an instructor. "You know the driver's side is the offside because it's away from the kerb."

"Yes. And the kerb-side is the onside. Compartments are numbered logically."

"That's right. Now, you've studied the location of every item carried in or on the appliance. Let's see what you remember. Where is the combi tool?"

Closing her eyes, she visualised the labelled diagrams of the truck. "I think it's . . . in that one." She pointed at a compartment.

Kel's voice gave nothing away, no clue if she was right or wrong. "Open it and see if you're right."

Thalia jumped off the table and walked to the offside compartment she'd named. A twist of uncertainty fluttered in her stomach. Having proclaimed how good her memory was, now, faced with proving it on something so different from cooking recipes, she wondered.

Was she as good as she'd boasted?
Only one way to find out.

She turned the handle and raised the panel. Nestled inside was the combi tool. Relief whooshed out in an excited breath. She turned to Kel, careful not to reveal too much elation.

He folded his arms across his chest and nodded. "Good. Now tell me where to find the one-and-a-half-inch hose."

Turning back to the truck, Thalia ran her fingers along the side and walked around until she found the right compartment. She paused, hand splayed over the panel, and checked the number against her mental list. "This one."

"Open it and see."

Kel ran through a dozen more items and each time she got another one right, the greater her confidence grew. Memorising items was as easy as memorising recipes. "I don't know what everything is used for yet, but I know where they all belong."

"I'm impressed at how quickly you learned them. Shall we move onto lesson two?"

Thalia bit her lip. Nico's accident had overtaken every other thing in their daily lives. "I'm sorry. I've read bits but I haven't had a chance to study much beyond what we covered in that first session." At this rate there was little chance she'd be ready to do the first training session, the progress marker Kel had negotiated for him to come to her book club.

For a big man Kel moved quietly, with athletic grace. Suddenly he was in front of her offering a hose that had been stretched out to dry. "I'm making this study session a practical one. Holding on to and directing the water from one of these isn't easy, especially for a wom— for a slightly built firefighter. But there are ways of positioning and anchoring yourself that will help."

Thalia took hold of the hose near the nozzle.

"Tip number one: you want to be as far back from the nozzle as you can and still reach the handle to open the water. We use a couple of methods, but because you're—smaller than most of the crew—"

She drew herself up to her full height and Kel grinned.

"Thalia, even in boots the top of your head barely reaches my shoulder. Admit it, you're small, short, petite."

"What has my height got to do with anything?"

"Only that you'll have to make adjustments

to compensate for your lack of inches. Dad always said that good things come in small packages when Mum complained about the same problem."

She allowed her gaze to trail down his body. "Small packages, hey? That doesn't sound promising."

Kel burst out laughing and picked up a length of webbing. "That's not something you have to worry about."

He used a girth hitch to attach the strip of webbing to the hose and held it up. "Use a piece of webbing strapping about two metres from the nozzle to reduce the nozzle reaction on your body. Then stand with your back to the nozzle, slip the strap over your inside shoulder and make a one hundred and eighty degree turn to the outside so the strap is anchored across your back, like this."

He demonstrated the movement in slow motion and then handed her the strapping. "The shoulder strap will be essential if you want to avoid bruises and use the hose efficiently."

Thalia lifted the strap over her shoulder, surprised by the weight of the empty hose. She turned as Kel had shown her and reached for the pistol grip.

"Hold the hose here and here." Kel stood behind her and positioned his hands over hers. "Take a wide stance, with your outside hand and foot forward, and brace for the water to flow. We always check that the lead firefighter is in position and ready before the water is turned on."

Thalia couldn't do more than nod. Not when Kel's body mirrored and cocooned hers, and his hands engulfed hers. Not when she felt she would combust with wanting him, needing him.

"I get it." The words dropped, sharp and needy, her chest tight as a drum.

If she wanted to draw her next breath she had to do something about this wanting him right now.

But Kel stepped away from her. "Sorry, Thalia. You must be exhausted after the past few days and here I am pushing you to haul around a heavy hose. Here, give that to me." He eased the strap from her shoulder and lowered the hose to the ground.

"No, I'm grateful for the time you've taken to show me. It's invaluable to see exactly how you do it. She looked away. If she left now, she'd never know if she could have—if they might ...

Grasping at straws, she threaded her fingers together. "I can't go yet. We—haven't discussed details of the party for your dad yet."

"No, we haven't. Events overtook our planning. But we can do it another time if you're tired?"

"I'm not tired—not too tired to . . ." Her eyes met his. Hiding her need to kiss Kel was beyond her. She'd have a better chance of stopping the Akuna River flooding than not looking at him, not wanting him.

"Not too tired to . . ." His gaze fell to her lips.

She leaned towards him.

"Do you want to talk about the party now, or—"

His voice dropped lower into the realm of sexy. He didn't complete the sentence. He didn't have to.

His voice, and the look on his face—like he couldn't stop looking at her, didn't want to stop— stole her breath. Blue eyes darkened with desire.

She knew what he meant, knew what she wanted. That *or* was beyond temptation.

Or was a necessity.

Or was every fantasy she'd indulged in. About Kel.

Only Kel.

He took her shoulders and leaned down. Stopped. "Thalia, are you sure this is what you want?"

For answer, she reached up and pulled his head down until her lips met his. She didn't want soft, or slow, or gentle.

She wanted the promise in Kel's dark blue gaze.

She wanted passion.

She wanted . . . him.

Kel's mouth touched hers, teased with slow, drugging kisses. She caught his lower lip between hers, caught the taste of his mouth and, fuelled by years of pent up desire, surrendered to the moment.

Zeus barked, the bark that signalled company just before a door opened. Voices rose in laughter, boots clattered on the floor.

Thalia and Kel sprang apart, breathing hard. She pressed her hands against the side of the truck, willing her legs to hold her up. Hormones on an exultant feminine high can-canned through her.

Kel's kisses hadn't met her fantasy.

Kel's kisses had gone beyond her wildest dreams. And if he didn't kiss her again, and soon, she'd . . .

"Kel, are you in here?" Dodge Myers stuck his head into the garage.

Kel took a deep breath and walked around the front of the truck. "Yeah, I'm here. Just running Thalia through some training. Reckon you'll have a tough time beating her at the next training session on *Find the Whatever*."

Thalia retied her hair tie, pressed a hand against her stomach, and walked around the front of the truck, plastering a smile on her face. "Hi."

Dodge grinned at her. "Is what Kel said true? You're going to whoop the lot of us at our own game, hey?"

"Kel was good enough to let me explore the appliance and its contents, but I really should be getting back home. I need to let my parents know how my brother is." And she needed to put some distance between her and Kel before she gave away how totally not-calm she was. Before she reached for him again. She moved towards the door.

"How's Nico doing?" Dodge stood aside to allow her through.

She stopped, remembering that her family had still to thank Nico's rescuers. "No change, not until the doctors bring him out of his coma. Thanks for your help in rescuing him, Dodge."

"I didn't do much. Just stood around with a hose looking heroic. Kel was the one who crawled through Nico's car and stabilised him, and kept him company until the paramedics arrived."

Thalia looked at Kel. "You didn't tell me that."

He shrugged. "No reason to. It was a team effort freeing Nico."

"Did he—was he conscious when you found him?"

***

Abby's warning, *don't share any details*, raced in, screeched to a halt and took up position front and centre in his mind, kicking up its heels like a chorus line dancer in the spotlight.

Don't share, don't share, don't . . .

"Barely, and he passed out when we lifted him out of his car."

Suddenly Kel knew he had to get out of the station, had to get away before he let slip more details. If he was Superman, Thalia was his kryptonite. If she wanted to know anything, all she had to do was press up against him, slant her lips across his and ask.

Or look at him with anxiety and dread in her big brown eyes.

Her teeth caught the quiver of her bottom lip and refused to give in to the emotion.

That flash of fear for her brother, the hint of vulnerability, firmly controlled, tugged at Kel's gut.

With superhuman effort, he tore his gaze from hers. "I've got a lot of work to catch up on. I'll take it home to avoid interruptions. Good work, Thalia. See you around. Dodge, I'll relieve you at midnight."

He caught a glimpse of surprise, hurt, and then anger flickering across her face before he made it into the kitchen and closed the door. After the heated kisses they'd shared, she had every right to expect better from him. Instead, he had deliberately turned his back and walked away.

Damn, that was a slap in the face for her.

But his brain had come up with zilch else he could do. Stuck between the proverbial rock and a hard place, he'd rejected her. And right at this moment, he hated himself for it, hated the gag order from Abby, hated the whole lousy timing of everything.

Dodge's wife, Tessa, was seated at the table cradling baby Tilly and watching him. "Ouch. And here I was thinking you were Mr Smooth of Bindarra Creek. Losing your touch, Kel."

"What are you talking about?" He reached behind her chair and took a bottle of water from the mini-fridge. Had Tessa seen him kissing Thalia? Impossible. They'd been on the far side of the truck. But if she hadn't seen anything, why that crack about *Mr Smooth*?

"I might not be a former police officer like my husband, but I know a woman who's just been thoroughly kissed when I see her. And you, my friend, have lipstick on your cheek."

Kel's hand rose automatically.

"Ha, got you. That reaction confirms it."

Kel slumped onto a chair. "I'm making a hash of things."

"You like Thalia . . . more than you've liked any other woman you've dated. What's the problem with that?"

"That *is* the problem. I can't." He knew he couldn't, shouldn't, and yet he did. He liked Thalia . . . a lot.

Why did I kiss her?
Because I couldn't not kiss her to save

myself. And now I've hurt her and stuffed up everything.

"Can't what? Like her? Kel, you're not making sense."

"At this moment in time, any relationship between Thalia and me is a no-go zone. Just drop it, Tessa."

Tessa nudged his arm with her elbow. "If you tell me why."

"I can't. Maybe later, but not now."

Dodge opened the door and stood blocking the entry, an odd expression on his face. "Thalia's gone. It's safe to come out now." An unspoken question hung in the air—*what the hell have you said to her?*

Weighed down with guilt and more than a little self-loathing, Kel looked up slowly. "I don't suppose I can convince you to drop the topic of Thalia?"

"And let my wife have all the fun? No way."

"I thought not."

Dodge pulled a chair from the table, turned it backwards and sat with his arms folded across the top. "Unless you can give me a damned good reason why you just gave Thalia the brush-off."

Tessa shook her head and stroked a finger across Tilly's forehead. "He's behaving like a giant clam."

Kel shoved his fingers through his hair. "It's

complicated."

"Thalia and complicated don't go together so . . ." Dodge's gaze narrowed. "Complicated since when? Nico's accident?"

The tension in Kel's jaw ratcheted up another notch. He would hold to his promise to Abby and not say anything, but Dodge had been with him at the scene. If anyone could guess the cause, it would be him. He looked at Dodge and dipped his head in a single, slow nod.

"Ah, so that's the way it is. Bad luck, mate."

Tessa looked from her husband to Kel and stood. "What is it I'm missing here? Seriously! You strong silent types and your spooky, unspoken communication. Tilly and I are going home to more interesting company."

"I'll walk home." Dodge bent and kissed Tilly's forehead and Tessa's cheek.

Kel stood and pushed the chair in. "I'll walk you out, Tessa. Dad and I are going to the pub for a meal. I'll try to catch a few hours of sleep before I come back at midnight. Later."

Chapter 14

Kel and his father entered the Royal Hotel amid a rising tide of loud voices. "Pretty busy tonight. I'll go see if there's a table out the back if you want to grab us a couple of drinks."

"The usual?"

"Yeah, thanks." Kel edged between two large groups and stepped down into the al fresco area, a fancy name for the beer garden. Outdoor space heaters lifted the temperature in their immediate surrounds, but not enough to justify the crowd occupying the outside tables.

Kel scanned the area twice. On the big screen, purple-shirted rugby players battled men in green for possession of the ball. Most faces were turned towards the screen and no one made any sign they'd be moving before the game ended.

Kel was about to go back inside when he realised Paddy Cullen was sitting alone in the back corner. A twinge of guilt flittered through his mind that he'd somehow overlooked him.

Paddy waved him over. The Vietnam veteran had become more sociable in the past couple of years, but still preferred his own company most of the time.

"Hi, Paddy. I almost missed seeing you back

here. Looks like the light above your table has blown."

Paddy picked up a light bulb sitting in the ashtray, held it up and inspected it and then set it back down. "Nah, I reckon this one will work okay. Right after I leave."

Kel chuckled. Paddy was up to his old tricks. "Don't like the bright lights, hey?"

"Give me shadows over spotlights every time. Packed out tonight for the game. Lot of green in this lot. You're welcome to join me, if a table's what you're looking for."

"Thanks, Paddy. Dad and I thought we'd have a quick meal. I didn't know half the town would be here tonight, but it won't be the quick dinner we were after. Can I get you a beer?"

"Yeah, mate, a schooner of mid-strength. Dave knows what I drink."

"I'll get you that beer and let Dad know you're here." Kel took a step, but Paddy lifted a hand towards him.

"Kel, before he comes out, how's your dad doing? I heard about the redundancy, but I've been up prospecting in the hills for the last couple of weeks. Just got back this afternoon or I'd have called in to see him before now."

Kel took hold of the back of a chair and leaned on it. As little as a week ago his answer would have been negative. A week ago Thalia hadn't yet worked her magic on his father.

Or on him, but their parting didn't bear remembering.

"Dad's not bad, actually. Better than you'd expect."

"I wondered. Must be coming up to the anniversary of your mum's death. His redundancy couldn't have come at a worse time." Paddy swirled the last half-inch of beer in his glass before draining the contents.

"Tell me about it. It's his sixty-fifth birthday on the twenty-sixth of the month."

"Humph, just a young fella. I'll be seventy the day before."

"Seventy, hey?" Maybe Dad's almost-shared birthday with Paddy was the answer to one of Kel's problems. "Mate, would you help with a bit of subterfuge? I've been trying to work out how to get Dad to his birthday and retirement party without him knowing it's on, and I reckon your birthday could be the way to go."

Paddy shrugged. "You're gonna ambush him? Sure. Reckon I can invite him out for a drink beforehand. What time's the party?"

"Can I let you know the details later? We're still planning it. The bowls club won't be available for functions after that fire, but maybe the CWA hall will be. Nice and handy for that drink together."

His father appeared beside Kel and set a tray holding three beers on the table. "Good thing you were standing there, Kel, or I wouldn't have spotted you. G'day, Paddy. Saw Kel chatting to you and brought you a beer to commiserate. Has he talked your ear off yet?" He took a chair and sat with his back to the other tables.

Paddy chuckled, a low, almost subterranean rumble that led to a bout of coughing. He thumped his chest with a fist and exhaled a wheezy huff. "Too many bloody ciggies in 'Nam. Have a seat, Kel, and take a load off your feet."

Kel took the seat against the outside wall and raised his beer, first to his father, and then to Paddy. "To the birthday boys."

His father lifted a glass and eyed Paddy over the top of a slim head of foam. "You too, eh, Paddy? How many?"

Paddy drank a mouthful and set his glass on the table. "Seventy. Starting to slow down a bit, but damned if I'm ready to curl up my toes. Gotta live life to the full. Hey, mate, you'll have to join me for a celebratory ale or three nearer the date."

"For sure."

Kel watched the two men talk, nonsense sprinkled with reminiscences, and occasionally joined in until their meals arrived.

There's definitely a spark of interest in Dad since Thalia showed up at home.

His father pushed the salt and pepper shakers close to Paddy. "I ordered a roast special with the beer when I saw you, Paddy. Hope you like pork?"

"Love it, thanks, Keeg, mate. I was just thinking, you missed out on the 'Nam draft, didn't you?"

"Yep. I was lucky. I was only eighteen in 1972, and four months later, they scrapped the lottery."

Paddy shook his head and snorted. "As if calling the bloody thing a *lottery* makes it sound better than what it was—sending young men off to a war we should never have stuck our noses into." He stabbed the air with his knife. "And now the government hardly wants to know about us, and whinges about pensions and stuff. Makes a man feel useless. Makes me angry."

Kel felt the outrage pouring out of Paddy, saw the anger in his eyes, felt the frustration in the white-knuckled grip on the knife.

He recognised some of the same negative emotions his father had carried around for the past four years.

Surely there was a way for men like his father and Paddy to continue contributing within their community and to maintain their dignity through service. Their experience alone was worth . . .

Kel's head rose like a hunting dog scenting its quarry. His gaze narrowed on Paddy cutting into his dinner with sharp, angry slashes, stabbing a piece of meat and chewing fiercely. Paddy had experience in the field, observation skills, and knew how to blend into the background. Underestimated and often unseen by a younger generation, the army veteran-cum-prospector would be perfect.

If he agrees, I can kill two birds with one stone.

"Paddy, how would you like to give the Fire and Rescue Service a hand?"

Paddy flicked a wary gaze from Kel to his father. "Sure. What do you need?"

"Have you heard about the arson attacks over the past couple of weeks?"

"Course. Most everyone's talking about the fires and wondering who the lowlife is who's starting them."

Kel lowered his voice, even though the chance of being overheard amidst the hubbub of the game on the television was remote. "We need your observation skills next time there's a call-out."

Chapter 15

"Thalia."

With difficulty Thalia forced eyes sticky with salt and sleep to open. Weighed down by exhaustion and hurt and a bare two hours of sleep, she was curled on her side, cocooned in the doona. If only she'd fallen asleep before dawn lightened the sky.

"Thalia?" Mama would call again and then, if she didn't respond, tug down her covers.

"This isn't like you to sleep in. Are you sick?" The bed dipped as Mama sat on the edge and laid the back of her hand against Thalia's cheek and forehead. "You don't feel like you've got a temperature."

Thalia tossed an arm over her eyes against the light of morning. "Just tired, Mama. Between worrying about Nico and trying to study on top of my regular jobs . . ." She rolled the other way and threw the doona back. "I'm coming now."

Mama stood and set about making the bed before Thalia was fully upright. "You've got bags under your eyes, Thalitsa. This is not a good look. Maybe you leave the study for one day, hey?"

Thalia stretched her arms high over her

head, unable to stop a loud yawn. "Maybe I will."

"I'll make coffee while you shower. And then you tell me about your three visits yesterday." Mama plumped the pillow with unusual force before tossing it on the bed.

Thalia straightened the pillow and drew the bedspread over it, smoothing a wrinkle before she stood and met Mama's gaze. Guilt spiked through her, at her selfishness in going straight to bed when she got home from the fire station, guilt that she hadn't thought about her parents' anxiety to hear how their son was doing. Guilt that she'd thought only of Kel's dismissive goodbye and her own sense of betrayal.

"Nico's the same. No change, but I talked to him and told him everything will be fine and that we love him."

Mama exhaled an audible breath. Her mouth softened, quivered, and she sank onto the newly-made bed. "Good."

Thalia sat beside her mother and took one hand between hers. "I'm sorry I didn't tell you that last night. I—just needed to be alone, to sleep."

Mama patted Thalia's hand and sniffed. "It's tiring, worrying about those you love." She stood slowly and walked to the door. "And those you love and who love you but don't yet know it."

Heat raced up Thalia's cheeks. She knew exactly what her mother meant, but it was mortifying that Mama could read her sadness and anger and broken dreams so easily.

"Get dressed and then come eat. You're fading away, Thalitsa." Mama closed the door behind her.

Thalia padded down the hall to the bathroom she shared with Nico. She gripped the edge of the sink and took back every frustrated remark she'd ever made about having to share with her brother. Towels hung over their railings, the non-slip mat was neatly aligned in front of the shower, and the cabinet doors were closed, just as she'd left them yesterday. If Nico came home, if Nico recovered, she'd never say another harsh word to or about him.

Splashing water over her face led to a wet pyjama top and a sharpening of her headache. Knowing the remedy lay in sleep, knowing she didn't have that luxury, Thalia swallowed a couple of tablets and stepped into the shower. Hot water eased her muscles, but nothing would ease the hurt of Kel's behaviour.

He hasn't changed. He's still Mr Love-'em-and Leave-'em. How stupid was I to think he'd changed? To think I was different?

She thumped the tiled wall, feeling the power of anger welling inside her. From now on, she'd have nothing more to do with Kel.

What about his father's party?

"Grrr." She dressed quickly, pulled her hair

into a high ponytail, and ran down the stairs to the kitchen.

"Here, Thalitsa. You have bright eyes now. That is good."

Telling Mama her bright eyes were anger with Kel would do no good. Telling Mama she wouldn't see Kel to finish planning the party would be like a red flag to a bull. Once a job was started, she and Nico had been taught to see it through, no matter any personal cost.

"Papa asked if you know where Keegan Jones' party is to be held? He wants to look at the kitchen set up and see how much we need to do here beforehand, and what we can do there." Mama set a mug of coffee in front of Thalia and leaned on the bench top.

As much as Thalia didn't want to see Kel again, organising the party was her responsibility. So she'd be business-like, professional, and throw a fire blanket over her raw emotions to get the job done.

And after today? What about the Fire and Rescue?

She wrapped both hands around her mug and sipped the thick Greek coffee she loved. *After today, I'll have nothing more to do with him. As for the Fire and Rescue Service, and my bet with the fire captain?*

She had no idea, no plan, and a head full of

confused emotions.

***

Kel looked over the roster he and Lou had put together earlier in the day. With Paddy, as well as Roman and Ty on board observing the crowd at the next fire—and Kel was certain there would be a next time—they had a good chance of catching the arsonist. All that remained was to let the Bindarra police know, and then wait.

Always waiting.

He turned off the computer screen and picked up his hat. Might as well see Abby and Riley at the police station while the details were fresh in his mind. He strode through the front door of the station heading for his car and all but ran Thalia down.

She grunted, an *oof* that was more surprised than hurt.

She's here. She came back.

Relieved to see her, overjoyed at her return, he grabbed her arms and steadied her.

Hope that she wanted to talk to him, that the lines of communication were still open may have led him to hold her closer than was wise.

But when had he been wise around Thalia?

She'd come to him, fallen into his arms . . . He may have smirked if he hadn't felt so glad to see her.

Her gaze rose and he felt his lips stretching, forming the shape of pleasure that he had another chance to make things right, to explain as much as he was able to.

She took a step back and looked up. Her gaze met his, and fried him with one sizzling, *get-your-hands-off-me-or-lose-them* look.

Hope shrivelled, died, and the ashes blew away before he uttered a syllable. His hands dropped from her arms.

Thalia hadn't forgiven him. She wasn't about to forgive or listen to pathetic half-stories.

"If you have time, Mama wants me to finish going over the plans for your father's party." Was her tone frosty, or was glacial a more accurate description? White-hot or frostbite-cold, either way, he deserved her anger.

Sad that he'd botched things—badly—with Thalia, Kel struggled to sound normal. "I've got time now if that suits you."

"Fine. Can we sit over there at the bus stop?"

"Wouldn't you be more comfortable inside the—" He gestured vaguely towards the station.

"I'd prefer to sit outside." She turned on her heel and strode the short distance down the road towards the bus shelter.

Kel followed, feeling foolish, feeling bereft—of her smiles, of her joy, and of the possibilities he'd thought lay ahead with her. He sat next to her, elbows on his knees, hands hanging loose between his legs. Not quite touching her, close enough to touch if her mood softened. "What do you need to know?"

She slid along the bench, creating a metre-wide gap between them. Crossing her legs at the ankles, she opened a notebook and tucked a strand of hair behind her ear. Her glorious hair was pulled up tight into a bun, stabbed with pins to tame its wildness into submission. "Numbers for a start, and venue. Papa said he doubts the bowls club will be repaired and available in time so he wondered about the CWA hall."

A lone pin stuck out a short way from her bun and he fixed his gaze on that. "I've been a little slow inviting people. Can I get back to you on how many?"

"Of course. If you want to give us a list of invitees, we can do some of the invitations as people come into the café if that will help. And the venue?" Her gaze was fixed on the notebook on her lap. The blue and white cover was pristine, and her neat handwriting covered barely half a page.

"You mentioned the CWA hall. I'll have a chat to Florrie Miller this afternoon and see if it's available on the twenty-sixth."

She made a brief note and then took a printed page from the back of her notebook. "These are menu suggestions. Mama asked if you could choose three or four main dishes, and tick as many entrées as you'd like. Papa included a cost guide on the back of the page. When you've made your selection, please drop the list into the Cyprus Café and we'll take it from there." Carefully avoiding any contact with him, she held the page out.

In the past, Thalia had treated him to snark with a sprinkling of sarcasm, but this brusque, business-like attitude was new. New and unnatural and he hated it. He had to keep her talking. If she left, it was over. If she left, he had as much chance as a snowflake at one of his call-outs.

"What do you recommend?"

"Everything on there comes recommended. You've tried most of the dishes at some stage so you know the quality of what we offer." She closed her notebook and tucked it inside her handbag and stood. "Thanks for your time."

"Thalia, I—"

"I've got everything I need from you, Captain Jones. We look forward to catering your father's party. And after that, I don't want to talk to you again."

"That will make for a boring book club meeting."

She tilted her head back and clutched the straps of her bag. "I release you from that bet. It was silly and simplistic and I can't imagine what you could contribute to our evenings."

***

Kel stood in front of her. Maybe he didn't mean to block her way, but between the bus shelter and the tree and him, Thalia was surrounded.

A dull flush of red filled his cheeks. "I can explain about yesterday if you just give me a chance, Thalia."

"Explain?" She gripped the strap of her bag more tightly.

Do not throw it at him. Do not hit him with it.

"What else could you possibly have to say? You kissed me and then, clearly, regretted it. I knew it, your friend, Dodge, knew it. That *goodbye* was the Kel Jones' special love-'em-and-leave-'em line. I got the message."

Even Dodge had seemed surprised by Kel's tone. He'd looked at her with sympathy and she'd wanted to crawl under the truck and curl up like an echidna, all bristly defence on the outside, daring anyone to approach. Instead, head held high, she'd wished Dodge goodnight and left.

It had hurt though, like the sting of a thousand Wait-a-While prickles on her skin. In the silence of her bedroom, with her arms clutching her stuffed toy Snoopy dog to her breast, she'd vented her tears and her anger. She cried and raged and cursed her weakness.

And when she was done, a curious calm had settled over her.

And look at me now. I'm going all Medusa on him.

Or maybe it was the blood of great warriors running in her veins. "Get out of my way, Captain Jones, or—"

"I didn't mean to—but when you asked about Nico I—" His mouth snapped shut and he closed his eyes. "Damn it, I can't tell you why, but Thalia, I'm sorry that I hurt you. It's the last thing I wanted to do."

"Fine. You're sorry and I'm leaving." She tried to step around him at the same time he moved aside to let her go. She moved the other way. He moved.

He took hold of her elbows and she flinched. Pain, sorrow, frustration—an emotion that could have been any or all of them flickered through his eyes.

She didn't want to think about it, or the way his hands on her felt so good, so right.

Kel wasn't right for her. He was *wrong, wrong, wrong*.

And Mama was wrong this time. Kel wasn't the man she wanted. She tugged one arm free and glared.

"Stand still. I'm trying to get out of your way, Thalia." He stepped around her until she had a clear retreat.

She turned to go.

Ty Devereaux stood beside the tree, watching them. "Is that some quaint country dance down this part of the country? It looks complicated."

Touching her tongue to the corner of her mouth, Thalia tried to assume her customer-friendly smile, the one she put on every day to cover a multitude of not-feeling-like-it moments. The smile that hung like her apron on the kitchen door. The smile she slipped on without a second thought. "Just discussing business, Ty. We're done here."

"Ah, about that *business*. Kel, I can't guarantee I'll be in town if there's a call-out tonight. Thalia, would you mind swapping rostered nights with me?"

She looked from Ty to Kel.

"I'm afraid I have no idea what roster you think I'm on, Ty. Kel, care to enlighten me what I'm not invited to?"

The hurt was back, bigger, harder, and weightier than before. Only this time she knew for sure . . .

Kel wasn't just rejecting her as a romantic partner.

Kel was rejecting her for his fire crew.

Chapter 16

The Cyprus was busy with the usual Wednesday crowd, but of Thalia, there was no sign. Kel stood in front of the register, guest list and menu in hand, and Stavros looking at him as though he had two heads.

"Here's the numbers for Dad's party, and I've picked some of the dishes Dad's tried so far. He loves Thalia's *moussaka* and her *baklava*, so they're definites." He waited for some response, any response to his mention of Stavros' daughter.

Stavros nodded. "*Nai, nai.* Her cooking is almost as good as my beautiful Thea's. Those are good choices."

Kel knew they were good choices. He had plenty of firsthand experience of how good both Thalia and Thea's cooking was. Food choices were easy. What was difficult was talking to Thalia— finding her, facing her, telling her as much as he could without breaking his word to the police. Convincing her to take another chance on him.

"Speaking of Thalia, is she around? She's usually out front on a Wednesday."

He'd held off coming in, knowing today was the one day he could be sure she'd be on the register. He'd given her time to cool down, but the unfortunate encounter with Ty had probably sealed Kel's fate. Why would Thalia listen to him after being left off the crew? Why would she trust anything he said, let alone let him talk? But he had to try.

"I need to talk to her."

Stavros half-turned towards the kitchen and Kel's eyes followed the movement. *There!*

He was certain he'd spotted her blue apron and dark curls through the narrow opening before the door closed. "Is she hiding out in the kitchen?"

"Kel, I don't know what you did, but you better fix it pretty damned quick or it will be too late. You like my Thalitsa?"

"Yes, but—"

"No buts. She made me take over the register when she saw you crossing the road. You want to lose her?"

"No."

"Then go out the back now and make things right with her." Stavros reached over and plucked the papers from Kel's hand.

They were crushed, much like he was feeling. But Stavros knew his own daughter, knew how her mind worked. And Stavros was happy for him to go out back and talk to Thalia.

Kel stepped away from the counter with no idea what he'd say to her, but a clear idea of how he wanted it to end. With his arms around her and his lips on hers.

"Just the man we needed to talk to." Senior Constable Abby Taylor leaned on the counter beside him. AJ stood a couple of metres back, hands folded in front of him, waiting, for what, Kel had no idea.

"Can I catch up with you later, Abby? There's something I need to do."

"I'm afraid not. We have a situation." She stood, immovable as the memorial on Main Street.

Kel frowned. "I'm a firie. You're the police. Why do you need me?"

"It's at the fire station. Please come with us."

Damn. My turf, my problem.

He glanced past Stavros to the kitchen door. It remained firmly closed, but he had no time to pursue Thalia now. He spun on his heel and led the way out.

A police vehicle was parked in the No Parking area near the corner.

"Hop in. We'll be quicker in the car." Abby held the rear door open for Kel and AJ got behind the wheel.

AJ did an illegal turn and headed off down Willow Tree Drive, two blocks down and one across. He pulled onto the concrete apron in front of the doors of the fire station.

Kel pulled on the door handle. "I can't open the door. It's stuck."

AJ glanced over his shoulder. "Doesn't work, Kel. You've gotta wait to be let out of the back of the police car. Hang on."

Abby got out and opened the door before AJ got there. "In the office."

Kel strode through the door and turned left into the kitchen. Gabe sat with his feet up on another chair blocking the entrance to Kel's office. For all Gabe's pose was relaxed, his expression was annoyed. A nasty scrape down his cheek ran into an angry bruise that darkened his chin. He cracked his red knuckles and Kel began to see what might have unfolded.

Through the doorway, Kel saw Connor rise from behind the desk. His attention was focused on someone out of Kel's sight.

Gabe put his feet down and stood, jerking a thumb into the room beyond. "We caught the little b- red-handed."

Kel stepped through the doorway and stopped, eyeing a high school student slouching in a chair in the corner. The boy's auburn hair hung in greasy strands above a school uniform with a torn pocket, shorts a couple of sizes too big, and a smirk. That smirk raised Kel's anger more than the boy's insolent gaze.

"Tell me what happened." He looked at the

boy who put his hands behind his head and leaned back as far as he could in the chair.

Connor sat on the edge of the desk and folded his arms. "Gabe and I decided to get on with the stocktake. While we were in the office looking for the list, we heard something bang in the stock room. Found Terry Parch filling his pockets with small items—" Connor pointed to a jumbled pile of items on the desk. "He was stuffing a can of oil into his backpack when we opened the door."

"Weren't me." The boy's tone was rich with ignorance and defiance and inflection that told them to *prove it.*

In the rudest of terms.

"How did he get in?" Their last safety and environment review was still current, but what if the boy had strolled in off the street and come through the front door?

He's got the attitude to try it.

"The catch on the back window had been jimmied and some messy knife work loosened the bars. Enough for Slim here to wriggle through."

Kel ran his gaze over the boy. *Scrawny rather than slim*, he'd have said. Underfed and scrawny, with a chip on his shoulder. A drop of blood fell on the floor, landing behind the boy's rundown joggers. Kel looked more closely. A trail of drying blood ran down the back of the boy's leg.

"Did you cut yourself when you scrambled

into the room?"

"Told you, it weren't me."

"Hmm, only whoever came through that gap seems to have cut himself. I'm guessing the bars were rough where they were ripped out of the wood. Rusty bars, they are. He might want to get an injection, and soon. Mighty nasty, the effects of a cut like that." He half-turned, as though to go, and then looked at the boy again.

"Weren't me." But Terry sat up a little and leaned forward. One hand slid down to the back of his thigh, coming away red when he took his hand away. "What effects?"

"Well, those bars have been there a long time. Probably gave way so easily because they're rusty. And a cut from rusty metal—" He shook his head and rubbed a thumb across his lower lip. "I don't like the chances of not getting—what is it, Connor?"

"Tetanus. It's known as lockjaw for a reason, Terry. It's incurable. You get tetanus from rusty metal, boy, and don't get the injection, you die. End. Of. Story. It's nasty. Only way to stop it is an injection, but you've got to be quick. But like Terry said, it wasn't him."

Kel leaned against the doorjamb and hooked his thumbs into his jeans pockets. "So Terry doesn't have to worry about seeing a doctor and getting an injection to save his life. That's a relief, isn't it,

Terry?"

The boy's eyes had grown wide and now looked more frightened than insolent. "Get me that injection now. I don't want to die."

"Tell us why you think you need it, and we'll see about that visit to the doctor." There should have been a hard edge to Kel's voice. In his head it sounded hard, but it came out encouraging, friendly-like. A voice a frightened boy might trust, believe, respond to.

"It was me. I cut my leg breaking into that store room. Now get me that injection." His voice rose, broke, and fell away on a gulped breath.

Kel stepped away from the door and Abby and AJ stepped into the room. Abby took the boy's arm. "Terry, we're going to take you to the station where we'll get a doctor to come in and give you a tetanus shot. Then we'll ring your parents and when they arrive, you'll be charged with break and enter."

"Old folks won't care. I don't want them there. Just get me that shot."

The police officers led Terry away, and Gabe joined Kel and Connor in the office. "Clever move. Didn't think anyone would get the little brat to confess."

"Anyone would think you were used to dealing with angst-filled teenagers." Connor rubbed his stomach. "That kid got in a couple of good punches. Hit Gabe on the chin and me in the breadbasket. Ducked like he was used to being in a brawl. It took both of us to frog-march him in here and make him sit."

"Yeah, he's a scrapper all right." Something about the teenager reminded Kel of Thalia. Not his rudeness or his insolence, and certainly not his appearance. In looks, they were nothing alike.

But that force of personality, their determination, and the will to make the world bend to a different, more accommodating shape—that, they had in common.

Kel headed for the coffee machine, filled it with water and turned the power on at the wall. "I feel sorry for Terry. From what you were saying, it sounds like he doesn't have a great home life."

"Careful, Kel, appearances can be deceiving." Connor took three mugs from the cupboard and set them on the draining board.

"I get that, but it might not hurt to let Abby know before she interviews his parents."

Gabe huffed out an audible breath. "I'll do it. I'm closest to the phone, and it was me he clobbered first. I'll call Abby now and tell her what we saw. Might help his case."

"Thanks, Gabe." Kel spooned coffee into the filter, paused, and then added an extra spoonful and switched the machine on. A Greek coffee was out of the question. He'd become fond of the strong black with fine grounds in it. He'd become fond of the woman who made it just how he liked it. But there was no chance of heading back up to the Cyprus Café for a coffee, and no chance of talking to Thalia.

With a mug of coffee in hand, Kel went to investigate the damage and make a call to the glazier. He set Connor the task of inventorying everything in their storeroom. "Just in case Terry was passing stuff to someone on the outside before you guys caught him".

A report would have to be written and the damage to the storeroom window repaired immediately.

As if we haven't got enough to worry about with an arsonist setting Bindarra Creek on fire without having to deal with a security breach at the station.

Chapter 17

Papa pushed the kitchen door open and left it ajar. He stood where he could keep an eye out for customers through the opening into the café while he talked to Thalia. "Are you going to tell me what that was all about, why you pushed your Papa into taking your place?"

"Don't you think one argument with the fire captain in front of customers was bad enough? I didn't feel like being polite to him today." She picked up a bowl of salad, tore off a strip of plastic from the wall-mounted dispenser, and stretched it over the food.

"Thalitsa, why are you pushing him away? I thought you liked Kel, but you've been sad or angry all week."

"Why shouldn't I be? Nico's in hospital in a coma and *that man* is behaving like . . . like . . ." She muttered under her breath, a Greek curse Papa had washed her mouth out with soap for uttering when she was a teenager. She still couldn't bring herself to utter it aloud in his presence.

"Like what? Has Kel done something to you?" Suspicion and concern and love fought one other in Papa's voice and rose like a tide of red in his face. Papa would do anything for his children, and everything to protect them.

"No, Papa. He's done nothing."

Nothing that I didn't want him to do.

The memory of how that *study session* had ended still stung. Rejection stung, but it wasn't wrong.

Undesirable, unpleasant, unworthy of him. But not wrong.

"Kel saw me through the doorway—I'm sure of it. And he didn't come into the kitchen. He couldn't be bothered trying to talk to me." Twinges of guilt pricked her conscience like spatters of hot oil from the pan. She wasn't blameless when it came to Kel's reluctance.

I told him I didn't want to see him again, and now I'm complaining he did what I asked.

"Oh, Thalitsa *mou*. Is that why you make this angry-sad face? He *was* about to come to you, only Abby and AJ took him away before he could."

"Took him? What, like arrested him? Why?" Thalia's stomach muscles contracted like they used to before she burst off the starting blocks in the school races. Sick with nerves, adrenaline, and fear she wouldn't live up to her reputation as the school's top sprinter then, now, she feared for Kel.

What did he do?

Kel might be a heartbreaker, but a lawbreaker didn't fit the man she knew. Or thought she knew. Those odd fragments of unfinished secrets haunted her.

I didn't mean to . . . I can't tell you why . . .

What was Kel not telling her? What had he done that he hadn't meant to do?

He's not a lawbreaker.

Questions chased one another through her mind, heads down like dogs following a scent. Except Thalia had no idea where that trail might lead.

"They mentioned the fire station. I think something happened there."

With an impatient tug, she loosened the ties of her apron and reefed it over her head. "I've got to go and find out what's happening."

"Why? You just said you don't like Kel and now you think he's in trouble, you want to run to him. Aieeee . . . me, I will never understand the mind of my daughter."

"I won't be long, promise. But I have to know he's okay."

Two blocks in Bindarra had never seemed far when she walked them. But running along Main Street, worried about Kel, worried about why she cared what happened to him, the blocks stretched ahead like a five-kilometre cross country race. She'd bolted from the kitchen, her pace too fast for the distance and her lack of training since leaving school.

Breathing hard, Thalia turned the corner onto Wattle Drive and stopped, chest heaving and hands on her knees.

One block ahead, the fire station squatted like a hunched gnome, guarding the police vehicle on the concrete driveway. From this distance she couldn't see anything, couldn't hear, couldn't know. She set off at a slow jog.

Two uniformed officers appeared, Abby and AJ, escorting a third person to the car.

A shorter male in school uniform.

Not Kel.

Thalia's silly, traitorous heart picked up the beat. *Not Kel, not Kel, not Kel.*

She reached the shelter of the new bus stop and waited, watching to see if anyone else emerged from the fire station. Car doors slammed shut and the police car made a U-turn. It drove past her and turned right onto Willow Tree Drive.

Adrenaline left her body and she sank onto the seat. As if the police would arrest Kel.

What was I thinking?

That assumption was as silly as . . . the idea of Nico being arrested for having his car accident.

Sillier. She could almost smile at the silliness now the police had driven off—*without Kel.*

She folded her hands in a white-knuckled

grip in her lap and shivered. Running out of the café without a jacket was even crazier. She'd never been so thoughtless, so why now? Why get upset at the thought of Kel being arrested? If it had been Nico the police were coming for, that would have been understandable. Nico was her little brother and, for all his random, misdirected energy, she loved him dearly.

But Kel? She didn't love him. She disliked him. Disliked, and was disappointed that he had behaved so oddly.

And therein lay her problem. Kel was never unkind, never mean, always charming. Except . . . somewhere along the way, their relationship had morphed into more than kind. It had changed into meaningful, into *hot*.

Before she knew what she was doing, she crossed the road and entered the fire station. Voices came from the kitchen, neither of them Kel's. And then she heard him on the other side of the back door. A one-sided conversation. Was he on the phone?

She reached for the door handle.

"Abby, I promise you I haven't said a word about your investigation to Thalia."

Thalia's hand froze. Maybe she stopped breathing. Her ears burned at mention of her name.

Investigation? Who was under investigation? Why couldn't Kel tell her?

"I have no idea what she was doing outside the station just now. Maybe she's coming to ask questions about her study notes. Do you want me to go out and ask her?"

Thalia sucked in a breath, quick, anxious, fearful. It dried her mouth, hurt her chest, and pained her throat.

I can't be seen here. He'll think I'm—

The door opened and she jumped back. Too late to run, too late to hide, too late to escape Kel's surprised expression. She stood her ground and squared her shoulders.

Kel held the phone in front of his mouth, and through the speaker, Abby's voice rang clear. "Do not mention the investigation into her brother, no matter what."

Kel glanced at the phone and back to Thalia. "Understood. I won't be the one to tell her." Then he ended the call.

"Hello, Thalia."

Chapter 18

Whatever happened now, Kel hadn't broken his word. Whatever happened now was in the lap of the gods.

"What investigation?" Sugar-coated in soft tones, Thalia's voice was steel, determined to have the truth from him.

He took her arm and led her to the wooden picnic table in the tiny courtyard between the station and the narrow street that ran behind the property. They sat side by side and Kel began.

"Technically, you heard that the investigation exists from Abby so I'm not breaking my word."

"Agreed. Why is Nico being investigated?"

He drew a deep breath, exhaled slowly, as though ordering his thoughts. "Near the site of Nico's accident we came across a hayshed that had been set on fire. Deliberately. An empty oilcan was found nearby, and a drip torch was found in the boot of Nico's car. The torch had his fingerprints on it. The police banned me from speaking about it to anyone."

"Including his family. How could they?" A tremor passed through her, and her head tipped back, her gaze sliding away from him, away from information that shattered her world. "They think Nico is the arsonist."

"Maybe. They have to check out every lead. His fingerprints on the drip torch are—"

"Circumstantial, isn't that the term? But it couldn't be Nico. He wouldn't do something like that." She bit down on her lower lip and shivered.

He'd been surprised by her sudden appearance, and then intent on finding a way to make use of the opportunity provided by Abby's mistimed comment. That had to be the reason he hadn't noticed how poorly dressed for the weather Thalia was.

He stood, shrugged out of his jacket, and draped it around her shoulders. Maybe his hands lingered a moment on her shoulders, but he missed her. Missed the bright possibility that had seemed to stretch ahead of them the night he kissed her. "Is that better?"

Gripping the gaping sides of the jacket, Thalia drew them together and nodded. "Thank you. The fire at the bowls club—Nico was in hospital when that one happened. Why are they still investigating him? It couldn't have been him." Certainty firmed her tone and her gaze connected with his. "Surely that fact wipes him off their list of suspects?"

"Not quite. There were differences in the execution of that attack to how the earlier fires were started."

"What does that mean?"

"It means the police know Nico isn't in the frame for that attack, but it doesn't mean he couldn't have set fire to the hayshed, or the maintenance building at the oval."

"Oh." The pitch of her voice dropped, just like his stomach had when Abby pointed out the obvious to him.

He waited while the details sunk in, guessing how much harder it must be for Thalia to accept. He'd had nearly ten days and still couldn't imagine the scenario Abby had painted. One in which Nico Levonis burned down his town.

"And so they do what to uncover the truth?"

He spread his hands, palms up. "I don't know, Thalia. I guess they're waiting for Nico to wake and answer their questions."

"And you? What do you think? Do you also believe Nico is capable of these attacks?"

Kel shook his head immediately. "I don't believe he's guilty, but I'm not the police. They have their job to do, just like we have to get on with ours."

Confusion drew a frown on her brow. "When you say *ours*—"

"Your studies, and keeping watch for the real arsonist at the next fire. There will be another."

"You left me off your watch roster." Hurt

underlay her question, quivered in her words before she bit her lower lip. *His* Thalia hated showing weakness. "Was that because of Nico?"

That quiver tugged at his gut. If he could turn this around, if he could convince her to give him another chance, he vowed he'd never give her cause to feel sad again. "Yes. Partly."

Grateful they were talking again, treading carefully, Kel paused.

Man up and tell her why, tell her so she understands you care for her.

"But only partly. I didn't include you because I don't want you up close to the arsonist again. He's dangerous, Thalitsa."

"And you think you have the right to choose for me, to send others into that danger and not let me make my own decisions? Ty, for instance. It's because he's a man, isn't it? He's only a recruit like me, but you trust him to watch. Why can't you trust me too?"

"It's not about me trusting you, but I can't trust that I won't focus on you instead of fighting the fire. You distract me, Thali, more than you know."

She turned to face him, one hand slapping her breast. "I distract you? But I thought you weren't interested in me after—"

The dramatic gesture drew his attention, demonstrating how right he'd been to leave her off

221

the roster.

"Did you really believe I would treat you so badly after kissing you?" The idea hurt, but it made sense of her reluctance to talk to him. It made too much sense.

"Don't answer that. Of course you did. I want you to know, that night, I didn't trust myself not to blurt out the truth when you asked about Nico. But Thali, there's more to it than that. I bolted. From you and how you make me feel. What I was running from was myself. When I kissed you—"

"Please get your facts straight—I kissed you."

Had she leaned towards him, just a little? He was sure his thigh felt the heat of hers, his cheek, the warmth of her breath. That small degree of unbending gave him hope they might yet work through this.

"When *we* kissed, I started—feeling."

"Captain Love-'em-and-Leave-'em." Her voice was soft, but the nickname was harsh. Was that what others thought? What Thalia thought of him?

He turned away and looked at the ground. Had he hurt other women by his *three dates and move on* approach?

And yet . . . *And yet—I was afraid of getting close. Afraid of loving and losing that love. Like*

Dad.

He wouldn't let that fear dominate his life any more. Not when Thalia was still here and listening, talking, helping him. He owed it to her—to them—to lay it out for her.

"Caring for someone leaves you open to getting hurt. Things—*life*—happens, and people I love, people I care deeply about—they've gone in the blink of an eye."

"Your mum."

"And my grandparents. Mum's death hurt so bad, but watching what it did to Dad was—" His throat tightened around a ball of grief he'd buried deep inside, so deep he thought he'd dealt with the pain, his anguish held under that lump of grief while he looked out for his father. "It was like losing him too."

He sucked in a breath of cold air, feeling it race all the way down to his lungs, expanding, filling, displacing the fear he'd held in for four long years. *A breath of fresh air, that's what Thalia is.*

"Thali, in the interests of full disclosure . . . I'm scared of letting you get close to that pyromaniac because I'm afraid of losing you too."

Her hand reached for his and squeezed.

"Just so you know, I'd prefer you didn't lose me either, but I'm not fragile. I won't break." Her thumb rubbed across his hand and he gripped her fingers tighter.

"I know. You're tough and strong, but will you please do this one thing for me?"

Her tongue peeped out, touching the corner of her mouth. "If I get to ask for one special favour too."

"Anything. What is it?"

"I'll let you know when I've decided. Whatever I ask for, when I ask for it. Do I have your word?"

"You have my word."

Chapter 19

Kel's phone rang and his beeper went off a few seconds later. Blinking to clear sleep from his eyes, he picked up both, reading the message while he answered the call he'd been expecting for the past week.

"He's struck again." Lou's voice had an edge of excitement.

"Where?"

"At the high school."

"I'll meet you there. I'm on my way."

His gaze darted to the clock. After midnight.

He pulled on his protective gear, laid out and ready every night since they'd come up with their plan, and pressed his speed dial for Paddy Cullen. Lou would alert Ty, and Connor would let Roman know they were needed.

"Paddy, you right to come out, mate? It's at the school."

"I'll be there in five."

Tonight they would catch the arsonist.

Kel tamped down his impatience and drove the short distance along Wilgara Avenue to the school, turning into the driveway that ran up beside the oval. Impatience led to mistakes and missed opportunities, and he'd be damned if he let the arsonist slip through his fingers again. He parked on the grass verge beside Lou's car and jogged across to join her.

Flames licked up the joists of the derelict, century-old building. A wall of heat rolled over them. One-hundred-year-old wood crackled and spat. Two melting wheelie bins sagged beneath the veranda while lines of yellow fire raced into wooden walls.

In Kel's memory, winter in the building had snap frozen his fingers when westerly winds whistled through the cracks. Cracks that now drew in oxygen to feed the hungry flames. An orange glow flickered through the windows of the second storey. "Do you know if the building's empty?"

"No idea. The Education Department was debating whether to keep it or start a new block from scratch." Lou checked her phone for updates, a job Kel would be doing now if he'd been on duty tonight. "The crew's almost here."

The fire truck turned into the schoolgrounds. Kel scanned the immediate area. No bystanders, no shadowy figures, nothing but crackling flames and hissing as the fire took hold.

If he hadn't been looking for them he'd have missed Ty and Paddy arriving on foot, one after the other from the front of the school. They took separate paths and stopped in shadows some distance from the burning building.

The truck pulled up beside Kel and Lou. Connor and Gabe jumped out.

"Lou, you're in charge." Kel took out a hose and attached it to the water supply. Gabe picked up the nozzle and tucked the hose into his body. "Ready?"

"Ready."

Lou took up the position behind Gabe and turned to Kel. "I'll work with Gabe. You two check if the outside stairs are holding and then break down the door."

Kel dredged back more than a decade for details. If memory served him, the old block was set out with a central hallway and three rooms either side. Nearest the door, a small office lay to the right. He pointed to the left side. "There was a storage room on the left. If the block's empty, there shouldn't be any chemicals stored there."

But if it hasn't been cleaned out?

"Take it slow just in case."

"Gotcha." Connor climbed the stairs slowly, checking each tread before he put his weight on it. A hose trailed behind them like a monstrous python waiting to be fed.

The fire had gone up inside the old wooden wall. Out here, it didn't look too bad, but when they broke down the door, it would be a different story.

They reached the veranda and Kel breached

the outer door. A wave of fierce heat rolled through the opening. Smoke swirled ahead of them, closed around them, dense as heavy fog. Kel dropped into a crouch and peered ahead. Through his visor, through the smoke, through the layers of heat. Flames licked a doorway on the right. He signalled to Connor and moved aside.

Connor opened the nozzle and water gushed through the smoke, around and through the doorway. A flood of water consumed the flames, but it was the storeroom on his left that concerned Kel. He signalled his intention to Connor and prepared to break in.

As he turned his boot clipped the storeroom door. It opened on a narrow sliver of darkness.

It's not locked.

Kel pushed the door wide. His headlamp lit dull metal shelving. Metal shelves empty of cleaning products and chemicals. Empty of explosive materials. Empty of any sign of fire.

He gave Connor a thumbs up and Connor redirected the nozzle. They advanced down the hallway past the old office, checking for flares, checking for embers. At the second doorway, Kel's old classroom, a chunk of ceiling crashed at their feet.

Kel looked up, pointed. Just visible through the smoke, flames outlined a ceiling beam. Glass popped outwards as windows burst.

Connor aimed the water along the beam. Kel followed the line of fire. It had raced up past the windows. The rubbish bins, the source of the fire, had been tucked in below those windows. The damage might be limited to this section of the building.

Revealed in the smoky light from their headlamps, black water ran in dirty streaks down the walls, dropped in fat, ash-filled plops from above, left dirty tracks down Kel's visor. He clomped down the hallway through filthy pooled water to the veranda and looked down. He gave Lou an all-clear signal, and she returned it.

Whether they'd saved the building would be determined by assessors. It was enough to know they'd beaten this fire.

##

Lou turned from stacking gear and dusted off her hands. The police were standing by their vehicle, red and blue lights running across the roof.

Kel closed a compartment and looked around. "Have you seen our observers?" A few people still hung around but there was no rush, no excitement, no arrest taking place. Despite all their plans, this was the result. Nothing.

"They stayed in the shadows."

"Good. No point giving away our plan if our arsonist is still hanging about." Kel coughed. His eyes stung, and his lungs stung, and the lack of an arrest stung, weighing heavy on his mind. It was disappointing. Frustrating. "D'you know if they saw him? I still think they're our best chance of catching him, even if it hasn't yet happened."

"Agreed. Debriefing back at the station?" Lou pulled out her phone and texted. "I've told Ty to join us there. Connor, can you let Roman know the same?"

A short time later, the crew plus their observers gathered around the table in the station kitchen. Gabe set a tray of steaming mugs of coffee in the middle.

Kel looked around at the long faces. "Okay, so we didn't catch him tonight, but did anyone see anything?"

Paddy frowned and set his mug down. "There was movement in the southeast corner, over towards Fred's garage, but damn it, Kel, I couldn't get an ID on him. Pretty sure it was a man though. Dark clothing, but he disappeared when the fire engine turned up. Almost straight away."

"If that was our man then he's not getting his buzz from watching the action. What else? Ty, anything?"

Ty shook his head. "Nothing my side of the blaze. I thought there'd be more folks come out to have a look. Two couples with school age kids, and one young bloke I saw with a backpack. I didn't recognise him, and he headed to the truck stop long before you got the fire under control."

Kel scratched his stubbly chin. "Which could mean something or nothing. Some arsonists just wait for the action to begin and then leave. Others want the whole show. Did you see if he was still there when you left the schoolgrounds?"

"He was. Looked like he was waiting to thumb a ride. Want me to let whoever's on duty at the police station know?"

Kel's gut feeling was that the backpacker was simply passing through town, but the tired group sitting around the table needed something for the extra hours they were putting into the job. "Yeah. Probably worth getting Riley to talk to him."

Lou opened a notebook and entered the date and time. "While tonight is fresh in your minds, what do we know so far?"

Details were offered and noted, times and places and ignition methods, and summaries were drawn up.

Ideas ran out, yawns were hidden—or not—behind hands, and Kel rubbed his eyes. "It's late. There's nothing more we can do tonight. Thanks, everyone. We'll get this bloke yet."

Kel locked up and drove home slowly. Something about the list Lou had made bothered him, but he couldn't pinpoint it. He was tired and his smoke *hangover*, the name Dad had given it early in Kel's firefighting career, fogged his brain.

After showering, he lay in bed and ran through the methods and times, thought about how each of the fires had begun.

Nothing.

Dammit, why can't I see it?

As the eastern sky lightened, he gave up the struggle and closed his eyes.

Chapter 20

The hospital visitors' room had been redecorated in shades of spring green and bright white. Bright, like Doctor Jess Frobisher's smile as she looked at Thalia and her parents. "Nico's recovery is progressing well. We're ready to bring him out of his induced coma."

Mama clasped her hands to her chest and closed her eyes. "*Dóxa to theó*, thank you, God, at last."

Thalia sat forward, joy turning cartwheels in her chest. Unlike her shocked response the day Nico had been brought into the hospital, this time, she'd had time to research, to prepare questions, and to get this interview with the doctor right. "Should we be concerned about the amount of time he's been in the coma? Are there likely to be problems?"

"Given the severity of Nico's injuries, two weeks isn't unusual. He's still got a long way to go, and the break in his leg will mean he won't be dancing any time soon, but we believe he's well on the way to recovery."

Papa didn't look convinced. This morning he had stood at the top of the front steps and talked about installing a ramp. "Will my son be okay?"

Doctor Frobisher nodded. "Mr Levonis, it

will take time. He'll need physiotherapy sessions for a while, but Nico will recover. It's possible he may experience partial amnesia, but his memory should gradually return."

"When can we talk to him?" Thalia knew that was the burning question for all of them now they had been given the good news. "Can we see him now?"

Doctor Frobisher shook her head. "I'd suggest leaving your visit until mid to late afternoon. Give him a chance to adjust to what's happened. It's possible he won't remember the accident at all. That happens sometimes."

"Thank you. Papa, Mama, let's open the café, serve lunch, and share the good news. We'll come back around four o'clock, if you think that's not too early?" She looked for confirmation from the doctor.

Doctor Frobisher handed her a business card. "Call me on this direct number when you're ready to come in, but I expect that time will be fine."

They left the hospital and walked to where Papa had parked the car. Smoke hung on the air and, through the trees to the south, Thalia glimpsed the school.

There's another arson attack they can't pin on Nico.

A fierce joy filled Thalia's heart. Nico was

clearly innocent of the last two fires. The police would have to see how unlikely it was that he'd set the other fires—*any fires.*

How long would it be before the police learned he was awake and came to interview him about his accident? How long before she knew why he had a drip torch in his car? Wanting to hug him and box his ears at the same time, Thalia climbed into the back seat and settled for wrapping her arms around her waist, holding in her relief, her fear, her joy.

Little brother will soon be home.

Papa drove home along Court Street. As they passed between the vacant block and the Bowling Club, Thalia's gaze was drawn to Kel's house. His ute was in the driveway and she had a sudden desire to talk to him, to share her good news. Kel didn't believe Nico was the arsonist either.

She hung onto that thought over the next few hours as they served meals and told their friends about Nico. She hung onto it while they drove to the hospital, buoyant with hope. She hung onto it all the way into Nico's room, until she saw Senior Sergeant Morgan and AJ.

Then she lost it when she saw the pain on Nico's face, and his grip on the hospital-white sheet.

"I can't remember." Nico's voice was raspy,

uncertain, anxious.

Thalia stepped between the police officers and her baby brother. "The doctor said Nico might have partial amnesia for a while. Please don't push him for answers now."

Riley cast a frustrated look at Nico. "When the hospital advised us Nico was awake, we were hoping we could wrap up our investigation."

Thalia felt the same frustration. And anger. It rose like a cresting wave. Nico was being hassled over something she knew in her heart he couldn't have done. "I want Nico's name cleared as much as you do. More. He didn't set any fires. When his memory comes back—you'll see, there'll be a simple explanation for everything."

Riley turned a sharp-eyed look on AJ. It questioned how in the hell an outsider knew about the investigation and promised disciplinary action. As Nico's friend, AJ would be the most likely source of her knowledge.

Thalia understood all that and spoke before Riley could ask. "I overheard a comment Abby made. I wasn't meant to hear, but I know what you're thinking and it isn't possible. Nico isn't your arsonist."

Mama gasped and sank into a chair. Papa blustered, red-faced and disbelieving. "You think this of my son? How dare you?"

AJ took a step towards her father. "Mr

Levonis, we don't think Nico is the arsonist, but we have to—"

Riley put a hand on AJ's shoulder. "We have to investigate any links to a crime, and Nico's accident happened near a fire we're sure was arson. It's possible Nico saw something. That's why we need to talk to him. I'm sure you understand how important it is that we follow every possible lead to catch whoever is doing this."

Thalia searched Riley's expression for any clue. Did he believe what he was saying, or was it just police-speak? She glanced at Papa. The red tide of his anger receded from his cheeks. He looked— older. Older and tired, but calmer.

Riley continued. "We'll leave you to talk with your son, but if he remembers anything about the accident, if he saw anything, please let us know immediately." He handed a business card to Papa who stared at it as though it was written in a foreign language.

"Let me know if I can do anything for Nico." AJ held out his hand and shook Papa's before he followed Riley from the room.

Thalia turned back to Nico. His eyes were closed and a frown she thought looked like he was in pain drew his brows together. She stroked his forehead. "Oh Nico, what did you see? What have you got yourself into?"

Slowly, as though they were heavier than

eyelids had a right to be, Nico opened his eyes. For the first time in two weeks, Thalia looked into her brother's eyes.

"Hey, Thalia."

Pressing her lips together, she blinked away tears. This was a happy time, a good time, a time for joy, not for tears. Not even happy ones. "Hey, Nico."

Nico's raspy voice was all it took to bring their parents to his bedside. Mama gushed, took hold of his good hand and cried. Papa swallowed and took in several noisy breaths and patted Nico's shoulder.

Thalia resisted the desire to press for answers. They would come, or not, if Nico's memory returned. For now, Nico was awake. It was enough. "It's good to have you back, Nico."

***

Kel stepped back, put the lid on the pen marker and considered the detailed summary of each of the attacks written on the white board. "There has to be a pattern here. Something we're missing."

Lou closed her notebook and leaned back in Kel's chair. "If we discount the fire at Angus's place and the hayshed for a moment, the others all occurred in Bindarra."

"Do you think there are two firebugs?"

Lou put her feet on the desk. "Ignition

methods suggest a different mind at work. The fire at Angus' place could have been started by a cigarette butt. We didn't find evidence to conclude it was deliberate so let's set it aside for now."

"Okay. But the hayshed fire was deliberate, and we found a drip torch nearby." Kel rubbed the back of his neck. "Let's focus on—"

Lou's phone buzzed. She looked at the message and stood. "Sorry, Kel, Warren needs me. One of the twins—"

"No worries. Thanks for your help, Lou."

After she left, Kel made a coffee and carried it back into his office. If he didn't count his rising frustration, he'd made no progress by the time his stomach reminded him it was time for dinner. He pushed back his chair and carried the half-mug of cold coffee into the kitchen.

Two light knocks sounded on the door and he turned. Thalia stood in the doorway, a plastic container balanced on a manila folder on one hand. With the other, she pulled her red beanie off by its pompom and tucked a strand of hair behind her ear. Her cheeks and nose were pink.

"Is everything okay?"

"Everything is good. I've just come from the hospital. Nico is awake."

Kel considered that news progress at least. "That's great news. Does he remember the accident or—"

"Not yet. Riley and AJ were questioning him when we arrived. I hope he remembers soon though."

Kel kept a lid on his disappointment. For Thalia and her family, the main focus would be that Nico was getting better. "Coffee?"

"No thanks. I—wondered if you would explain something for me. If you're not too busy, that is."

"Come into my office. It's a bit warmer in there." He set a chair beside his at the desk and let her get comfortable. "What chapter are you up to?"

"This one." She opened her notes and pointed to a diagram of the suction hose. "With everything going on I probably missed something in the notes, but I can't see how this works."

Kel explained the mechanics of it. "We used this to fight the fire at the McGregor property. Sunk it into one of the dams and pumped from there."

"I get it now. Thanks. You know, studying has been a sanity saver while Nico was in a coma."

"I don't know how you do it." Kel tried to imagine focusing on some of the technical stuff while sitting at a hospital bedside. "I don't think I could."

"It was a distraction, but hard to concentrate. I sat with Nico and told him what I'd learned each night. Not that I think he heard me. When people are in a coma, it's like a deep sleep. I Googled it.

But it helped me to be able to talk to him."

She tidied her notes away and looked at the whiteboard. "Are you trying to work out who the arsonist is by studying the fires?"

He looked at the columns of facts. Black writing on white, but nothing about the attacks was that simple. He walked across and stood in front of the board, pointing to the second column. "Yes. Leaving aside the hayshed, we've had three attacks in less than two weeks. It's unusual."

"Such a short time. It's almost like someone is making a statement." Thalia frowned. "You know what's weird?"

"Tell me."

She moved to the map pinned on the wall and pointed at the location of each fire as she named it. "The three attacks are really close together."

"Everywhere in Bindarra is close. It's not a big town, Thalia."

"I know, but they're all near your house. Look." Her finger settled on the spot marking his home.

Kel slipped on his glasses and joined her, peering at the map. "You're right, but I don't know what that proves, if anything."

"Maybe someone's circling closer to you?" She did the *doo-do* soundtrack from the shark movie, nudged him with her elbow and grinned. "Got any enemies, Kel?"

She was joking. He knew she was joking, but the proximity of three arson attacks to his home prickled up his spine like an army of ants at a picnic. "Maybe there's one woman in town who I've pissed off, but she's more likely to fight fires than start them."

"Ha ha, Kel."

But that wasn't quite right. Thalia had started a figurative fire under him, one that had shocked and surprised him when she swept into his station and demanded to join the fire service. A fire that had burned through four years of grieving and lit an answering fire within him.

He pushed his glasses up on top of his head and took her shoulders. "Thalia, I want to make it up to you for the way the other night finished. I'd like to start again."

She tipped her head, looking up at him with a glint in her eye. "You can't change the past. Real life doesn't have a reset button. But you can choose how you go on from here."

"In that case . . ." He lowered his head, felt her rise on tiptoe to meet his mouth. Second chances were better than a reset. They meant he'd learned from the past and moved forward.

And second chances tasted sweet. Thalia's lips touched his and he lost himself in the wonder of her giving him a second chance.

Chapter 21

Thalia dished a serving of lasagne onto a plate and reached for the salad tongs. It was late in the lunch service, and she'd half-decided Kel wasn't coming in today when he stopped at the counter in front of her. Her heartbeat kicked up a notch, knowing he was here to see her. The idea was wonderful, and new, and still surprised her that *it* had happened at all.

He smiled the smile she'd thought he shared with everyone, the smile that turned her insides into wriggly, squirmy worms. The smile she knew now was hers alone. "Hi, *koukla.*"

"Ssh." She glanced around. Was Papa close enough to hear? "What do you think you're doing?"

"Did I say it wrong? I meant to say—"

"I know what you meant. Just—I haven't said anything to my parents. About us."

Kel's smile dimmed and twin furrows appeared above his nose. "Why not? Did I misunderstand what happened between us last night?"

"Of course not."

Kisses that blasted all my doubts into little pieces and left me wanting—everything with him.

"I just haven't had time to sit down and tell them we're—dating now."

A slow grin that somehow combined cheeky with smouldering chased away his frown. "I can't believe it. You stayed strong after Nico's accident, and you've faced fire and an arsonist and done what had to be done, but you haven't told your parents about us."

"It's been a busy morning."

"Hah. I reckon I've finally discovered the one thing you're afraid of."

Inside, her warrior queen woke up and grabbed her shield and spear. Battle cry on her lips, she felt the adrenaline surging through her.

Kel looked at her and nodded, as though her reaction was exactly what he was looking for. "Now she's back. Good."

"Who?"

"Feisty Thalia. Thalia who challenges me to do better every time. Thalia who has the courage to face down—"

Tongs in hand, she pointed them at him, daring him to say more. "I'm not afraid of my parents—just—careful about getting the timing right."

His gaze drifted to her left and his smile grew. "I'm happy to tell them. Shall I start with your father?"

Papa came to stand beside her and nodded towards the customer waiting patiently at the servery to collect his meal. "Enough chatting,

Thalitsa. You have a customer."

Thalia warned Kel off with a quick shake of her head and a look into which she threw dire threats and promise of retribution. "I'll do it soon."

She handed over the plate with her customer-smile in place. "Sorry for the delay."

Papa waited for the customer to leave and leaned on the counter, chat-ready smile in place. "So, Kel, what can I get for you today?"

Kel's gaze zeroed in on her, hunger and passion and fire in his eyes that proclaimed: *I've come for your daughter.*

She pressed her lips together at the idea, wanting to grin like a crazy woman, and shout her own news from the top of Mount Olympus.

"I think Kel's after some of our new carrot cake. Isn't that right, Kel?"

***

Kel scraped the last crumbs of carrot cake onto the fork and popped it in his mouth as Thalia set two cups of coffee on the table. "Rationing my intake of your cooking is going to take all my self-discipline. That cake was wonderful."

She took a seat opposite his in what she thought of as *their* booth. "I'm glad you like it, Kel. Your mother's recipe is really good, but I worried my version of it wouldn't stack up to your memory of hers."

He took her hand in his and squeezed gently. "Don't sell yourself short. You're the best cook I know. Mum was, shall we say, creative in her cooking. Her meals were culinary adventures. I didn't fully appreciate that until she was gone." A flicker of sadness shadowed his eyes.

Thalia turned her hand beneath his. Calluses scraped her skin and goose bumps ran up her arm. What would that roughness feel like on the soft bare skin of her belly? Warm hands and callused fingers making a new map of her body, a map only Kel would ever read. The whole idea of *getting lost* in Kel and making her own map of his body stole her breath.

Lost in sensual images of discovering each other's bodies, she didn't notice Mama approaching the booth.

"Finally. I was beginning to think you would never—"

Kel's pager beeped, Thalia's phone pinged, and the café phone rang within seconds of each other.

"I've got to go—"

"AJ texted. Nico's remembered—"

"Thalia, we go to the hospital now." Papa's voice boomed across the café. He shepherded two tables of customers to the outside tables with profuse apologies and a free slice of carrot cake as compensation and locked the door behind them.

"Come, we go and see what Nico has remembered."
He picked up his keys, Mama pulled a jacket over
her apron and they were gone.

Kel grabbed Thalia's hand, followed her
parents through the back door and helped her up
into the rear seat. He climbed in after her and held
her hand all the way to the hospital.

No one spoke.

The same question was surely running
through each of their minds.

What has Nico remembered?

Abby and AJ walked into the hospital right
behind Thalia and Kel. AJ carried a small video
camera and gave Thalia a smile. They filed into
Nico's private room and stood around his bed.

Doctor Frobisher looked around the group,
stopping at Abby. "Nico requested this meeting
with all of you, but please keep in mind that he's
still recovering from his injuries. Don't push for
more than he can give you today." She turned back
to Nico and smiled. "Ready, Nico?"

Thalia decided the doctor had a sweet smile,
and, from Nico's expression, her brother was
probably halfway in love with her. That was Nico,
in and out of love, and fancy-free.

Nico looked around at his family, and his
friend, AJ. Like the doctor, he stopped when he got
to Abby. "I'm ready."

Maybe it was Abby's uniform, neat and

official, or her police-neutral, tell-me-all-you-know expression, but Abby commanded attention. "As Nico agreed to, AJ is going to record what he says." She ran through the formal spiel about the recording and how it would be used, and then nodded to AJ.

AJ aimed the camera at Nico, the red light winked on, and Abby introduced Nico and gave details of day and time and the people in attendance. "Go ahead, Nico, in your own time. What have you remembered?"

"Most of it I think. I went to visit a friend, my girlfriend. She lives out of town on a farm off Mount Ingalls Road out Corella way."

Across the bed, Thalia heard Mama gasp and saw her grip Papa's hand. It would take a huge revelation to trump that news in her book. Thalia wanted to be a fly on the wall when that discussion took place after this interview.

"We went to a dance and afterwards, we—you know."

"Nicolaides Levonis, were you fooling around with that young woman?" Mama couldn't help herself.

Abby intervened. "Please, Mrs Levonis, not during an official interview."

Colour ran up Nico's face and Thalia felt sympathy for him. It wasn't easy keeping their love lives from their parents.

"I was driving home late, after midnight I

think, along the main road. There wasn't any other traffic and no moonlight, so when I saw the fire, it was the only light along that stretch of road."

Abby slid a question in when Nico paused for breath. "Just to be clear, you were on the Mount Ingalls Road travelling east, back towards Bindarra Creek?"

"That's right."

"And the fire, where was that?"

"I don't remember the name of the property, but it wasn't far from where I've been told I had my accident. I think I could take you there if you like?" A hint of uncertainty clung to his question.

Thalia suspected Abby picked up on it too.

"It's fine, Nico. Tell us about the fire. What happened when you saw it?"

Nico frowned and Thalia held her breath.

What if he only remembers bits of that night? What if what he remembers isn't enough to prove he didn't set the fire?

What if . . .

Kel drew her close, anchoring her and chasing away her fears. She leaned into his warmth, drew strength from having him by her side.

Abby gave Nico a gentle verbal nudge. "Nico? What did you see?"

He startled, blinked, as though his memory had taken him back to that night. "I pulled off the highway onto a bit of a gravel strip that ran out at a fence. There were three men watching a hayshed burning. Not doing anything to put it out. One of them held a drip torch. I think I recognised his face from the Corella dances, but I—" He lifted his uninjured hand and rubbed his temple. "I can't remember his name."

"Don't worry, it may come back to you later. Then what happened?"

Thalia watched Abby's face closely. *Does she believe Nico? Does she believe what he's telling her?* The senior constable's expression remained police-neutral, but her gaze stayed on Nico. A gaze that softened, encouraged, sympathised with his frustrated efforts to remember.

Behind the camera AJ nodded, smiled, seeming to will Nico to continue.

"They bolted when I pulled up. Dropped the drip torch and ran."

"Did you see a vehicle? A number plate?"

Nico closed his eyes and frowned. "I think—there were spotlights on a bar above the cabin. It was a dual cab. Dark colour. Flashy wheel trims." He shook his head.

Thalia leaned over and touched his cheek. "Nico? It's okay, little bro. Don't push it."

He opened his eyes at her touch. "I tried to put it out. I thought about you joining the fire service and what you said about doing something for the community. It felt right fighting that fire.

Did I put it out?"

Kel leaned towards the bed. "You saved the shed and over half the hay. The owner was grateful about that."

Nico exhaled an audible breath. "That's good."

Abby waited patiently and then asked, "How did the drip torch end up in your boot, Nico?"

"I didn't think it should be left lying around. I was going to bring it to the police station the next morning. I thought it might have fingerprints on it."

Thalia groaned. "Oh Nico. *Your* prints were on it."

"I only picked it up with two fingers."

Behind the camera, AJ's face broke into a broad white-toothed smile, startling against his dark skin. "They were the two prints we lifted off that can."

Kel's hand tightened on Thalia's waist and he turned to Abby. "You implied Nico's prints were all over the oil can."

"Did I? Perhaps you assumed that, Kel. Anyway, you didn't need to know there were only two. At the time, we thought we were lucky getting partial prints and a possible suspect."

Nico tried to sit up, but could only raise his head from the pillow. He looked from Abby to AJ. "You thought *I* was the arsonist?"

AJ shook his head. "No man, not me."

Abby intervened again. "We have to investigate every piece of evidence, Nico, and sometimes that means setting aside friendship and looking at the facts. Now you've begun to remember, you'll be a big help to us in catching the arsonists. Anything else?"

"That's all I remember."

A cheery rat-a-tat knock sounded before the door opened and Ishya appeared with a mug of tea. "Oh, I'm sorry. I didn't mean to disturb. I'll come back later."

Abby thanked Ishya and turned back to Nico. "What about your accident?"

Nico shook his head. "I don't remember much. I put the oil can in my boot and left. As soon as I turned onto the highway, a car raced up behind me and sat on my tail. Lights on high beam." He frowned and shook his head again. "I think it rammed me. Sorry. I don't remember the accident, except—" His gaze settled on Kel. "Were you in my car?"

Kel nodded. "I was. You told me you had something to tell just before you passed out."

Abby spoke in a low voice to AJ and then, "Interview ended at two-thirty p.m."

AJ turned off the camera. "That's my man. Always knew you were working for the good guys." He held out a hand.

"Thanks, AJ." Nico gripped AJ's wrist in

their own personal greeting.

Abby's lips twitched, but she stayed professional to the end. "Good work, Nico. We'll start a search for those men and their vehicle. If you remember anything else, no matter how small the detail seems, let us know. One last thing, what's your girlfriend's name and address?"

"Stella Langton. She lives at—" He frowned, the same frustrated, perplexed frown he'd worn earlier, and thumped the bed with his uninjured hand. "Dammit, I can't remember the farm's name."

"Language, Nico."

"Sorry, Mama. It's frustrating."

Mama's fingers trembled as she smoothed Nico's hair off his forehead. "I know, *agápi mou.*"

"Doesn't matter, mate. We'll find your girlfriend." AJ was still grinning as he followed Abby through the doorway.

Thalia understood that grin. She probably wore the same one. The grin that said *all's right now Nico's awake. All's right and Nico's not the arsonist.*

Chapter 22

Thalia pushed the front door open and stepped into the hum of activity in the CWA hall.

"Look out below." Penny Lane's voice came from the top of the ladder to Thalia's right just before a trio of streamers floated past her. "Sorry, Thalia. Bad timing."

"No damage done, Penny. Wow, this is looking good." Thalia set her cane basket on the floor and eyed the decorations. An African game park theme with cut out animals and big cats' eyes peering through crepe paper foliage.

Penny climbed off the ladder and joined her. "People want to make this party special. They like Keegan and sympathise with him about the forced retirement. Anyway, why should a number carry more weight than how someone performs at work? Just because he's turning sixty-five doesn't mean he's suddenly not able to do his job."

"True. I can't imagine Papa taking kindly to someone telling him he's no longer *useful* because he's reached a certain age. There were a few other workers who got notices like Keegan, weren't there?"

"Four or five, I think. Keegan's the only one

who's turning sixty-five. But the others are all fifty plus. It makes me angry how businesses treat mature-aged people. They don't care a fig about experience." Penny's usually pleasant expression hardened into anger.

"In Greece, there's a different attitude to older people. They aren't shunted off into homes for the aged where they're lucky if they get a visitor once a year. But here—"

"I know, although our Bindarra aged home is lucky to have caring people in charge." Across the room, a couple of staff from the retirement home were helping to set up tables and chairs.

"Penny, what is there to do in Bindarra Creek when people retire?"

"Good question. Short answer is, I don't know. Maybe it's something we as a community need to look at."

Now Nico had woken and was improving each day, Thalia had emotional energy to spare. It latched onto a nebulous memory, a promise she'd made before the accident but not had a chance to fulfil. "I offered to teach Keegan how to cook some of the dishes his wife used to make. I wonder—"

"Cooking classes? I like your thinking. Once Keegan's had his party, why don't we talk with a few people about possibilities? I'd like to be involved. Maybe the CWA ladies would offer the hall for classes."

Thalia picked up her basket. "I'll call into the bookshop tomorrow. We can talk more then." She wove between stacks of chairs and scurrying workers, calling out cheery greetings on her way to the kitchen. As the door swung closed behind her, it muted the sound of party preparations.

She set her basket on the central stainless-steel counter and checked the fridges were switched on and cold. Papa should be here any minute with the first load of food and she wanted the centre bench clear before he arrived. The back door opened with a squeak of hinges needing oil.

"The fridge temperatures are fine and—" She looked up, expecting Papa with the delivery of salads and desserts. Kel closed the outside door and smiled. "Good to know. Sorry I don't have anything to put in them."

Thalia slipped into his arms, reached up and kissed him. "Mmm, better than any dessert."

"And there's a new dilemma for me." He kissed each corner of her mouth and nuzzled her cheek.

"Why?"

"Because of the next time I kiss you—when I tell you your desserts are the best thing I've ever tasted. Nothing comes close to kissing you, Thalitsa, but nobody makes *baklava* like you do either."

"Mama does."

The back door banged open again as Kel dropped a light kiss on her head. "Mmm, but I don't want to kiss your mother."

Papa clomped in with a wide, shallow plastic box filled with disposable silver trays of dessert. "You better not think about kissing my Thea. You have your own Levonis woman. Pay her the attention she deserves and you'll never have time to think of another woman." He set the box on the counter and eyed off Kel.

Kel didn't release her. He held on tighter and kissed her forehead. "I don't want to kiss anyone else. Not when I have one of the two most wonderful women in Bindarra in my arms. How's that for diplomacy?"

Papa grinned and Thalia gave Kel a quick kiss on his lips before stepping out of his arms. "You're learning." She began unpacking the trays into the fridge. "Do you want me to wait here, Papa, or shall I do the next delivery?"

Kel slipped an arm around her waist. "Or I could do the next trip and bring the food here for you?"

Papa chuckled. "Just so long as you remember to put the food away before you kiss my Thalitsa and forget everything else."

Kel was the most wonderful distraction, but Thalia didn't want anything to spoil his father's party. "Papa, you know you can trust me when food is involved."

"Food, yes. When the captain of the fire service is involved—I'm not so sure." His eyes danced as he looked from her to Kel and she knew for certain. Papa was happy with her choice of partner.

For now, she and Kel were dating. Officially. Butterflies took off in her stomach and soared.

Maybe one day, she'd answer Kel's proposal with a *yes*.

But maybe only after he's practised asking a few more times.

***

As Kel reversed into the café's driveway from the car park at the rear of the shop, Paddy Cullen hailed him.

"Kel, all set for tonight?"

"Yep. You still okay to get Dad down to the pub around five-thirty?"

"All sorted. He thinks we're having a pub meal after and that you're joining us. What time do you want me to bring him over to the hall?"

"Just after six o'clock would be good. Everyone should be there by then."

Paddy rubbed his belly. "Can't wait. I'm hanging out for several helpings of Thalia and Thea's cooking. See you there."

"You and me both, Paddy." Kel followed his nose into the café kitchen where Thea was covering the last of several trays of a spicy beef dish.

"Kel, how come you're here and not my Stavros? Did he con you into doing his job? I'll give him—"

Kel raised both hands. "I volunteered. It gives me an excuse to see Thalia again before the rush of the party." He grinned and snaffled a broken piece of slice from a plate of bits. "And the chance to taste-test another dish before tonight. Mmm, I see where Thalia gets her skill from."

"No need to butter me up, Kel. I've always thought you were the man to keep up with my little Thalitsa. Keep up with her and keep her safe when she gets mad ideas in her head." Thea plumped down on a stool and pinched her apron into folds.

Keen as Kel was to get back to Thalia, he could see Thea was distressed. He had a good idea what it was. He'd seen her face, watched her fear when Nico talked about putting out the fire at the hayshed. He recognised a parent's fear for her child. "You don't like the idea of Thalia joining the fire service?"

"You're brave and I know what you do is important, but . . . I can't bear to think of my daughter in danger like that. Talk to her, Kel. If anyone can talk her out of it, it's you."

Kel kneeled on one knee and took hold of

Thea's hands. "Thea, I hate the idea of Thalia in harm's way facing a fire too, but do you really believe anyone could talk her out of anything she decides she wants to do?"

He'd made an attempt to dissuade her from the idea of walking the Silk Road and look where that had ended up.

With Thalia applying to join the Fire and Rescue service and me about to join the book club.

And with Thali in my arms.

Not all bad then.

"Will you at least try?" Thea's eyes were bright with unshed tears. She sniffed and drew an audible breath. Like Thalia, her mother was a strong-willed woman. "Please, Kel. I was so afraid when my Nico was hurt, and I'm afraid for my daughter. Proud of her, but afraid too."

"I can't promise I'll be any more successful than you, but I'll try talking to her."

"What's this?" Stavros banged the kitchen door against the wall and stood, arms folded. "First I walk in on you kissing my Thalia and now you're on your knees to my wife?"

Kel grinned. "I can explain . . ."

Thea stood and smoothed down her apron. "Don't be foolish, Stavros. And why did you interrupt Kel and Thalitsa. You know better than to walk in on a man kissing his—"

"I didn't mean to, but I had my arms full of

desserts. Anyway, why is Kel on his knees in front of—"

"Stavros. Come and kiss your wife hello and then get out front and see to our customers. We still have a few to serve."

Stavros smiled. Thea smiled, and Kel caught a flash of Thalia's *I-love-life-and-my-man* in the look in her mother's eyes.

He turned his back on Thalia's parents, making a small production out of checking the trays of *moussaka* were all secure in the box. Giving them a quiet moment in a busy day. When he judged the time was right he picked up the box and turned. "I want to thank both of you for all the work you've done for Dad's party."

"It's our pleasure, Kel. You can thank Thalitsa later too." Thea winked and Stavros grinned and reached for his apron.

And Kel thought how wonderful it would be if he convinced Thalia of the absolute perfection of the next stage of his plans.

Chapter 23

"He's coming. Everyone quiet." Kel moved away from the window and stood facing the front door. The lights were off in the CWA hall, but there was enough spill from the streetlights to see a ragged semi-circle of friends waiting to surprise his father. Nerves gripped Kel's stomach. His mouth was dry.

Dad's never liked surprises. What was I thinking?

The door opened, two figures stepped inside and Paddy's voice rose. "Kel said he'd join us as soon as he'd checked the fire extinguishers for the CWA ladies. Wonder where he is?"

The lights were turned on. Arms and voices rose. "Surprise!"

And Kel's father smiled. Not a tightening of his lips that was more grimace than smile. This was a full on, teeth-showing, eyes-crinkling *happy* smile. It bounced off Kel onto Thalia, and then his father moved forwards, hand outstretched.

"Kel, my boy, this is great. Thank you." He pumped Kel's hand and gave him something just shy of being a man-hug.

Thalia stood off to the side. "Happy birthday, Keegan." She reached up and kissed his cheek.

And then, to Kel's surprise, his father

hugged her. His depressed, standoffish, grieving father was hugging Thalia.

Kel was speechless.

He shouldn't have been. Thalia had already worked her magic, but seeing the pleasure on Dad's face just now was—

He shook his head. Thalia truly had a healing touch.

She stepped out of his father's arms, nudged Kel and whispered around her smile. "Don't just stand there. Welcome everyone and get the party going."

"Uh, yeah, thanks for coming, everyone. Bar's open, and entrees are coming out. We've got a lot to celebrate tonight."

Paddy clapped a hand on Kel's shoulder. "I didn't think it would be so easy to get him away from the pub. Do you think he suspected anything?"

Kel laughed. "I don't think so. Well done, Paddy. You deserve a beer for your effort."

"One beer?"

"Yeah, one beer and keep them coming."

"That's more like it." Paddy rubbed his hands together and headed for the bar, decorated with a mismatched mix of green palm leaves and cut-outs of African animals.

Penny walked up and gave Kel a beer and tapped her glass of wine against his bottle. "Love the theme. Is Africa your next trip?"

Kel swallowed a mouthful of beer. "I'm hoping it might be Dad's. He and Mum used to talk about visiting a game park to photograph the wildlife. Dad loves photography, but he hasn't touched his camera since Mum died."

"Thalia and I were talking about this very issue earlier. She said she'd offered to teach your dad to cook, and that got us thinking what there is to do in Bindarra once people retire."

"Not much. And the bad thing is, I'd never thought about it until Dad's redundancy notice arrived." Mum's anniversary had cast a long shadow over everything else. Kel knew his head-in-the-sand attitude had as much to do with self-preservation as his own struggle to cope. He'd struggled to think of his father hitting retirement age, struggled with the idea that time and the world kept turning.

Penny pursed her lips. "Most of us could say the same. It's a bit like giving to charity. We don't think of it until someone we know is affected."

Kel's phone vibrated in his pocket. He ignored it. If the beeper went off, he'd have to go, party or no party. "So do you think she means to start cooking classes?" It was the first he'd heard, but Thalia was a whirlwind when it came to getting things done.

Penny's gaze snagged on someone behind Kel. "It's an idea, but we didn't have time—"

"Kel." Thalia touched his arm. He looked down, expecting a smile, and saw her gripping her phone. Her expression was carefully controlled, but something was wrong. Funny, how much better he was reading Thalia's moods since he'd kissed her.

"Excuse me, Penny. I'll be back in a minute." He led her to a quieter spot away from the music, near the front door. "What's up?"

"Dodge rang my phone because you didn't pick up. The arsonist. He's at the council offices now."

Kel's gut tightened. His heartbeat raced with the thrill of the chase. "At last."

"Do you want to talk to him?" She offered her phone.

Kel took it. "Dodge, don't let him out of your sight. We're on our way." He handed the phone back, and then his voice rang out over the hubbub. "Fire Service personnel to me, now."

Like rivers drawn to the ocean, his team forged paths through the partygoers, and gathered around him – Lou, Connor, Gabe, Mandy, Roman. "It's on. Council offices beside Fig Tree Lodge. Connor, Mandy, bring the truck. Lou, Gabe, Roman, you're with me. We're going to catch that bastard tonight."

Ty stepped forward. "I know I can't operate the hoses yet but anything I can do?"

"Let Riley or Abby know. I'm heading

straight to the scene."

Thalia gripped his arm. "Can I come this time?" It was personal for her too. Fierce desire to be there when they caught the arsonist shone in her eyes, glowed in twin spots of colour in her cheeks. "I need to know. I have to be sure Nico is made safe."

Suspicion about Nico had made it as much her fight as his. But even knowing that, Kel had promised her mother he'd keep Thalia safe. And he wanted her safe. He wanted her as far away from danger as she would accept.

"Will you look after Dad and keep the party going? I promise you, we'll have more to celebrate very soon."

Warring desires to help—to go and to stay—battled in her eyes. "You promise?"

"I promise."

Kel led and his team flowed through the exit in his wake.

Connor and Mandy jumped into her VW and roared along the two-block drive to the station.

Kel led the others around the corner onto Willow Tree Drive at a fast jog. They pressed against the shadowed walls of the Ingalls Development building and looked at their target. Across the road, the ugly, low-set Council Chambers squatted on the corner of the main road through town. Behind, a magnificent Moreton Bay fig in the grounds of Fig Tree Lodge dwarfed the council building. The glow of fire on the underside of evergreen leaves seemed almost pretty.

"Gabe, Roman, go down the side of the BHC building and come in from the east. Lou and I will come in from the western side. With Dodge on the north, we'll catch this bastard in a pincer movement."

Nods all around and then the team split and crossed Mt Ingalls Road at a run.

Kel's chest was tight, his breathing, harsh.

As he and Lou came along the western footpath towards the rear driveway, he detected the tang of accelerant, heard a voice chanting, "Burn, you bastards, burn."

On the Fig Tree Lodge side of the fence, he caught a glimpse of Dodge hidden behind the fig tree. Kel and Lou waited behind the last panel of old fibro fencing and Kel signalled his intentions to Dodge.

"Lou, we go on three . . ." He raised three fingers high and lowered them one by one.

The last finger dropped.

Dodge jumped the fence, Kel and Lou charged down the driveway, and Gabe and Roman appeared from the eastern corner of the building. They converged on a dark-clothed figure holding an empty plastic fuel container.

"Got you." Kel and Dodge reached the short

hooded figure first. They grabbed his arms and Kel pulled back the hood.

"Kent Conway?" The balding head of the middle-aged clerk was shiny with sweat and flames glinted off a pair of thick spectacles.

Behind them, the fire engine turned into the driveway and Riley and Abby raced in from the street.

Kel and Dodge dragged their prisoner back to the fence line, out of the way of the truck. The rest of the team set to work, pulling out hoses, directing water onto the flames. The fire crackled, hissed, steamed.

Abby and Riley handcuffed Kent, but before they led him off to the station, Kel stopped them. "Why, Kent?"

Behind the thick lenses, Kent's eyes were huge, a faded blue amidst railroad tracks of red. He blinked owlishly and looked at Kel. "Your father would know why. He understands. He gets what it's like to have thirty-five years of loyal service in the council office thrown back in your face. Thirty-five years and that witch of an HR woman hands me a redundancy notice and a *don't-let-the-door-slam-you-on-your-way-out* smile.

"She said I was redundant like some piece of out-dated hardware. *Me!* I set up the technology department for this council. And kept it running despite cutbacks." Kent was breathing hard. His face was red and shiny in the flames of his anger.

"But why the other fires? The school and the sports oval?"

"Council owns the oval. Hit them where it hurts, in their hip pocket."

"Enough, Kel. We need to take him to the station." Riley nudged Kent towards the police car. The former council employee walked with his head high and an expression Kel thought looked like grim satisfaction with his handiwork.

Dodge folded his arms and shook his head. "I never expected our arsonist to be quiet Kent. I thought we were probably dealing with that Dare Club out Corella way."

"Yeah, although I thought maybe the school fire could have been the work of students. The rubbish bins are more their style." Kel turned towards the building. Thanks to Dodge's early warning, the fire was quickly extinguished and the crew moved onto post-fire checks.

Lou opened her protective jacket and flapped the edges in a *this-is-cooler* way. "Nice of Mandy to grab my gear on her way out. Kel, how about you get yourself back to your dad's party. We can finish up here and join you later."

Dodge agreed. "Tessa and I will be there soon. Just as well Tilly chucked up over her and she had to change her dress or I wouldn't have been here to spot Kent setting his fire."

"Tell Tessa—and Tilly—I'm in their debt. Thanks, everyone. See you all back at the hall." Kel strode across Mt Ingalls Road and headed back to the party.

***

Thalia had the fidgets. The firefighters were off saving another building and she was stuck overseeing a party. Not that she was complaining. Tonight was a special night for Kel's father. It was more the feeling she wasn't doing her bit to help the town.

Her gaze fell on Keegan over by the bar, laughing with Paddy and a couple of older men. It struck her then that it was Kel who was missing out. Missing his father's birthday party because he was off doing his job. Doing his duty.

Protecting Bindarra.

It was Kel she should be feeling sorry for, not herself for missing out on the action.

Carrying a tray with the last of the *spanakopites*, she offered the platter to the group around Keegan. "Last one, Keegan. Lighten my load, won't you?"

"Never could say no to a pretty woman, especially one bearing food. Great food by the way."

"Plenty more to come. Mama thought we should hold off serving the main dishes for a little while and give the fire crew time to get back. Unless the fire is very bad."

But they would have heard by now if it was bad, wouldn't they?

She carried the empty platter back to the kitchen.

Her parents were adding the final touches to trays of meat dishes—sprigs of basil and rosemary and lemon thyme with little handwritten labels to sit behind each dish. Mama looked up. "Did you think the *spanakopites* were a little soft?"

"They looked fine, Mama, but I didn't taste them." Thalia's stomach roiled at the thought of food. Twisted and turned at the thought of Kel and the others facing yet one more fire.

"Thalia, we need to start serving these dishes now."

"Can't we wait just a little longer, Mama?"

The outside door opened and Kel stepped in on a rush of cold wind. "Mmm, smells great."

Mama looked up at him and shook her head. "If we wait any longer, the food won't be hot. I don't want to reheat it again. It strips the flavour out."

Thalia rushed into Kel's arms. She buried her face in his shirt. It smelled smoky and there were flakes of soot on his shoulders and a streak of black on one hand, but he was here. "Is it over? Did you catch him?"

"We did. I'll tell you about it shortly. Thea, Stavros, could you keep a tray of food for the crew. They may be a little while, but they'll be back."

"Sure, sure. We keep two trays for them. Go back to the party." Papa shooed them towards the door into the hall. "Thalia, go with him. We got this covered."

Kel picked up Thalia's hand and kissed the back of it, and then looked at her parents. "The arsonist has confessed. Nico's in the clear." Then he led her into the hall.

Thalia rose on tiptoes trying to see over the heads of the crowd. "Your father was over near the bar just before."

"I see him. He's still there with—surprise, surprise—Paddy. Come on."

They threaded their way to the bar, past folks asking about the fire. Kel tossed out brief assurances that all was well without stopping to offer details. He smiled and nodded and said, "Got to get back to Dad and keep this party moving."

Keegan looked a little merry, although Thalia wasn't certain. Maybe this was how he used to be. Kel's father had seemed much happier in the last couple of weeks than in the previous four years. "Did you catch him in the act?"

"We got him, thanks to Tessa running late for your party. Dodge spotted him from the lodge. He was setting the fire."

"Much damage?"

"Not from what I could see. It had barely had a chance to start. Dad, don't share this around yet, but—it was Kent Conway."

"Kent? Impossible. That man wouldn't hurt a fly." Keegan shook his head, looked away and back at Kel and frowned. "Kent? I can't believe it."

"He was angry about being made redundant."

Keegan gestured, a wide, slightly wild sweep of his arm. "The fool. *I* was angry about being made redundant too, but I didn't go about burning down council property. That's what this was about, isn't it?"

Thalia put a hand on Keegan's arm. "He must have been very upset to do something like that, and maybe he doesn't have anyone at home to talk to? Not like you. You're so lucky to have Kel."

Keegan looked at her, an arrested look of surprise. "Kent's alone, never married. His mother passed away last year." He drank a mouthful of beer and shook his head again. "Geez, I'd never have picked him as having the guts to do something like this."

"Not sure it's guts, Dad. More likely pent-up anger. He hates the council for putting him off. Maybe he's angry about his life in general."

Thalia looked from Keegan to Kel. A rush

of warmth, of tenderness, of love for both men surged through her. It should have surprised her, this knowledge of love.

But it didn't.

Even when she'd thought she disliked Kel—heat rose in her face at the insults she'd heaped on him—she hadn't been able to ignore him. How could anyone ignore Kel? He was the most *un-ignorable* man she knew.

"Keegan, would you take the first plate and get people started while the food is hot please." Not that Thalia wanted food. She wanted a quiet place and Kel's arms around her. But they would have to wait until the party was over. Unless . . . "I need Kel for a moment."

Their gazes connected, Kel nodded, and Keegan grinned.

"Come on, Paddy, grub's up. You were complaining you hadn't been fed. Now's your chance." Keegan and Paddy headed to the buffet table and picked up a plate each. Other guests followed.

Thalia tugged Kel into the tiny stage-side room and closed the door.

Kel perched on an old wooden desk, slipped his arms around her and drew her close. "You need me, hey? What do you need me for, Thali—Thalia? Sorry, I forget you don't like that name."

The desk was perfect for her plan. She

hitched herself onto it, bringing Kel's face almost on a level with hers, low enough she didn't have to go up on tiptoes to reach his mouth. "Actually, when you say my name in that low, growly voice—Thali—it's different. It's—like you want to kiss me and keep on kissing me. It makes me feel like I'm jelly and my legs go weak like cooked pasta and—"

"All my favourite foods."

"I thought *baklava* was your favourite?"

"Whatever you cook is. But my very favourite of favourites is the taste of your lips. The night you brought *baklava* to Dad, I wanted to kiss the honey from your lips."

"I knew that. But kisses lead to—"

"More kisses." He dropped light, feathery kisses from her ear to her jaw, and at each corner of her mouth. "Was it kisses you needed when you brought me in here, or am I being big-headed thinking you want to kiss me?"

"Not big-headed. I'll let you know when you are."

He chuckled. "I can count on you for that, can't I."

"Yes, but I needed—wanted to kiss you."

"Hmm . . ." He cocked an eyebrow. "Thali, Thali, Thali—shall I say it some more?"

She blinked up at him and whispered, "I've got the squiggly feeling in my stomach now."

"Then let me do something about it." He

tilted his head and, sliding a hand into her hair, gently pressed his lips to hers.

Chapter 24

One month later

Thalia raced into Kel's office at the fire station and waved a piece of paper under his nose. He didn't need to read it to know what it said. He could read Thalia too well to need it spelled out in black and white on mere paper.

She slapped the page down on his desk. "I did it. I passed the first stage of training."

"Knew you'd do it first time around. We'll celebrate tonight." Kel slid his arms around her waist and lifted her, kissing her with the hunger of a man deprived of his love for too long. A day without kissing Thalia was too long. A week without her was torture and no amount of physical exercise had changed the hunger of his body to know hers.

"The team will be grateful you're back."

She slid down his body until her feet touched the ground. "Have you been working them hard?"

In very short order she was going to feel just how *hard. Missed-you-in-a big-way* kind of hard.

"You'd better believe it."

She brushed her stomach back and forth across his body and he knew. Thalia was always one step ahead of him.

"Not so *hard* that you're too—tired to celebrate?" She walked her fingers over his chest and casually flicked open first one, then a second button.

"I'm ready to celebrate right now if you keep doing that." Longing made his voice growly with need.

She sat in his chair, spinning it in a lazy circle before he thumped both hands on the chair arms and stopped her. "Right here. Right now, Thali. Especially if you keep looking at me like that."

"Don't you want to know how your other recruit did?"

"Tell me." It was always better to let Thali tell things in her own way, in her own time. Patience had its own reward. He grinned.

"Ty passed too, of course. Now you have two more team members for call-outs."

"Unless we get a hazmat. You can't come on those until you've finished the second part of your training."

"I will."

"And while you were away the police confirmed the hayshed fire was the work of a member of the Dare Club, and they've arrested the three men who bumped Nico's car into fishtailing." If Kel had his way, the trio would be locked up and the key thrown away for several years. "Dangerous idiots, the lot of them."

"I'm relieved that's over, although Nico will probably have to give evidence when they go to trial, won't he. And speaking of Nico, there's one more piece of news before it gets to be *here and now*."

He picked her up and sat on the chair, settling her on his lap. He cocked one eyebrow. "Tell me quick. Clock's ticking—*tick...tick...tick...*"

"Nico's out of all but the leg cast and . . ." She grinned, a wicked, mischievous upward tilt of her lips and a naughty spark in her eye. "Nico's applied to join the Fire and Rescue Service too. Now you'll have two Levonises on your team."

"Double trouble." He tried to keep a mock-serious tone in his voice, but his focus was fast disappearing with every wriggle Thali made. Wriggle, slide, press against him.

Who am I kidding? She knows precisely what she's doing to me.

He lowered his head. She turned at the last moment and he kissed the corner of her mouth. "How's he at taking orders."

"Better than me. But it depends who's giving the order."

"And if you agree with them."

"Try me. Give me an order." Her voice was whisper-soft, seductive-sexy.

She held his face between her hands and fixed him with a look. Not her laser-look. This look—this incredibly intense and focused look—set his heart racing with joy. There was something new there, something he'd waited patiently to see in her eyes. Waited for her to share.

"Kiss me, Thali. Kiss me so I know you've missed me."

Her features swam in front of his eyes as she leaned close. Her breath mingled with his, her lips grazed his. "How about I kiss you like I love you? Because I do."

"I thought you'd never ask."

Epilogue

September 2020, somewhere near Tashkent on the Silk Road

"Look at that view, Kel. And the road—it stretches beyond the horizon. Oh, I can't believe I'm here."

"I always believed you'd be here one day, Thalia Jones. You picked a perfect honeymoon."

"Bet you never expected this would be the *special favour* I asked for." She stepped in front of him and turned, walking backwards. Still surprised, thrilled, excited—*stunned*—by the fact she'd finally agreed to one of Kel's proposals. He'd asked her five times before she agreed. "Do you remember the first time you proposed to me?"

"The first time? I think that was in September, right after Nico's arm cast came off."

"No, the first time was in the Cyprus Café. You were moaning around a mouthful of *moussaka* and, when I told you I'd cooked it, you proposed."

"See how smart I am. Even then, I knew you were the woman for me."

She mock-punched his arm. "That was your stomach talking. You just wanted to be well fed for the rest of your life."

"It really was delicious, Thali. But seriously, I knew you were the only woman I wanted, even when I thought I'd blown my chances. I just had to prove to you I was worth taking a second chance on. You didn't have a very good impression of me."

"Only because I didn't really know you. To my shame I looked no deeper than the man who had kissed every eligible woman in Bindarra. I let my prejudice blind me to the man in here." She stopped walking and set her hand over his heart. It beat with a thump-thump she loved listening to at night, her ear pressed against his chest. It beat for her. For . . .

"I have one teensy little question to ask and I want you to promise me you won't freak out."

"Aside from every time you come on a call-out, nothing worries me."

"About that. I've been thinking, now Nico's almost finished his training, maybe one Levonis in the Fire and Rescue is enough."

"True, especially now we have two Joneses on the team."

"Well, actually—you know that last fire we attended before we flew here?"

Kel looked at her with narrowed eyes. "What about that fire? What aren't you telling me, Thalitsa?"

"We had—three Joneses present."

"Three . . . three . . ." His Adam's apple bobbed up and down and he sucked in a deep breath. "Thali, are you . . . pregnant?"

She nodded. "I think that will have to be the

one and only time, at least until he or she is big enough to handle a hose."

Kel held her face and kissed her, slanting his mouth over hers in a fiercely sweet possessive kiss.

"I hope you're happy. It's happened a bit earlier than we planned."

"I'm happy, Thali. God, I love you." And then he dropped to his knees, splayed one hand gently over her still-flat stomach and rested his forehead beside his hand. "Welcome, little one. I can't wait to hold you."

Her eyes watered, but Thalia wouldn't cry. Not even tears of happiness. Not now she had everything she'd ever wanted in the world. "And I'm glad we're all walking the Silk Road and making memories together. I love you, Captain Jones."

The End

Thank you so much for taking the time to read my story, ***In the Heat of the Night***, which is part of the group writing venture - **Bindarra Creek A Town Reborn series**.

All reviews are appreciated.

Word of mouth recommendations have given me many wonderful books to share and I'd love it if you tell friends if you have enjoyed Kel and Thalia's story.

If you are able to leave a written review on your preferred e-platform, long or short, I would be very grateful.

~

Bindarra Creek A Town Reborn

Welcome to Bindarra Creek, a struggling country town where people work hard and love deeply. Set in the picturesque tablelands of New England, Australia, Bindarra Creek is a fictional, drought stricken community full of intrigue, adventure, drama and romance.

Life and love in a small country town has never been more challenging.

Bindarra Creek A Town Reborn series consists of eight romances written by eight Australian authors and published individually (beginning in July 2019).

In order of release:

Take Me Home – Suzanne Gilchrist (aka S E Gilchrist)
In the Heat of the Night – Susanne Bellamy
No Looking Back - Linda Charles
Worth the Wait – Annie Seaton
With Every Breath – Lauren K. McKellar
Stealing Her Heart – Simone Angela
A Twist of Fate – Erin Moira O'Hara
Promise Me Forever – Juanita Kees

~

To date there are three group writing venture 'series' set in our fictional small town of Bindarra Creek all written by best-selling Australian romance authors. Our latest series is A **Town Reborn.** A collection of short romances**, Bindarra Creek Short & Sweet,** was released in January 2019 and our first series, **A Bindarra Creek Romance,** was released during 2015/2016.

All books are available as ebooks, some also have paperback versions.

Each series has one theme running throughout, while every romance depicts the changing lives of the townsfolk as our small town begins to grow and thrive despite the dramas of everyday life.

Bindarra Creek Short & Sweet is comprised of:

What's in a Kiss – Linda Charles
My Forever Valentine – Sandie James
Pearls and Green Beer – Susanne Bellamy
Full Circle – Annie Seaton
Date with Destiny – Erin Moira O'Hara
A Letter From the Queen – Lee Christine
Love's Sweet Challenge – Suzanne Gilchrist (aka S E Gilchrist)

The Widow Maker – Lauren K. McKellar
Out of the Blue – Noelle Clark

~

Books in the first **Bindarra Creek Romance series:**

Bindarra Creek Makeover - S. E. Gilchrist

Shadows of the Heart - Lee Christine

Second Chance Love - Susanne Bellamy

The CEO Mechanic - Sandie James

Reach for the Stars - Kerrie Paterson

Home to Bindarra Creek - Juanita Kees

Stolen Sanctuary - Stacey Nash

Tempting Fate - Erin Moira O'Hara

One More Day - Linda Charles

The Vine - Lauren K. McKellar

The Ghost of His Past - Simone Angela

Joanie's Dilemma - Marianne Theresa

Buckley's Chance - Noelle Clark

For more info on Bindarra Creek Romances, please visit

www.bindarracreekromance.com

Acknowledgements

With special thanks to Kyle Hamilton for answering numerous questions about firefighting and the Fire & Rescue Service

And to Efthalia Pegios, for Thalia's Greek phrases.

Huge thanks also to Annie Seaton for her ongoing friendship and eye for detail in bringing this story to you.

*

BIO

Born and raised in Toowoomba, Susanne is an Australian author of contemporary and rural romances set in Australia and exotic locations. She adores travel with her husband, both at home and overseas.

Her heroes have to be pretty special to live up to her real life hero. He saved her life then married her.

A hybrid author, she is published with Harlequin Mira/Escape. A popular guest speaker, she presented the keynote address at the Steele Rudd Pilgrimage, was a guest speaker for the Dynamic Life Speakers Series for U3A, and has been invited to speak in libraries, book clubs, and to community groups.

Social media links

a. Facebook
   https://www.facebook.com/susanne.bellamy.7
b. Twitter
   https://twitter.com/SusanneBellamy
c. Website
   http://www.susannebellamy.com/books-by-susanne-bellamy.html
d. Pinterest
   http://www.pinterest.com/susannebellamy/

e. Goodreads
    https://www.goodreads.com/author/dashbo ard
f. Bookbub
    https://www.bookbub.com/authors/susanne -bellamy

Head on over to my webpage and find out more about all my rural series and other stories.

*